Keeping Sam

by

JOANNE PHILLIPS

This novel is entirely a work of fiction. The names, characters and incidents portrayed in it are the product of the author's imagination. Any resemblance to actual persons, living or dead, or events or localities is entirely coincidental.

Mirrorball Books
An imprint of Bostock Publishing

www.bostockpublishing.co.uk

Paperback Edition 2013
ISBN 978-0-9573094-1-8

Copyright © Joanne Phillips 2016

Joanne Phillips asserts the moral right to be identified as the author of this work. All rights reserved in all media. No part of this publication may be reproduced, stored in a retrieval system, or transmitted, in any form, or by any means, electronic, mechanical, photocopying, recording or otherwise, without the prior written permission of the author and/or publisher.

Typeset in Sabon, printed and bound in the UK by Lightning Source
Cover design by Blondesign

Keeping Sam

by

JOANNE PHILLIPS

Mirrorball Books

More Books by Joanne Phillips

Can't Live Without
The Family Trap
Cupid's Way

Flora Lively Investigates:
Murder at the Maples
A Date With Death

Chapter 1

The first time Kate Steiner learned to walk she was eleven months old; the second time, she was two months past her thirtieth birthday. Kate had no memory of those first ambitious steps, cruising around low-level furniture, every adult in a six-foot radius poised to catch her when she fell flat on her face. What she did know, twenty-nine years on, was that learning to walk was probably a damn sight easier when your legs were short and chunky, and your centre of gravity only a foot above ground level.

'Come on, Kate. You can do it!'

Not a caring mother with wide eyes and outstretched arms, but a young physiotherapist called Joseph, with muscular arms that bulged underneath a tight T-shirt as he guided Kate towards the end of the parallel bars.

'I can't,' she told him. 'It's impossible.'

'You know better than that.' His tone was admonishing, with a hint of tease. 'Nothing's impossible – haven't I told you that already?'

'Once or twice,' Kate grumbled, gripping the bars with shaking hands. She shifted her body to the left, taking the weight on her elbow, then swung her right leg around, planting her foot on the blue mat as firmly as she could. Sometimes her limbs felt as though they were borrowed, grafted on, as though she'd been in an accident instead of in a coma, and had been rebuilt, part by part, but that something had gone slightly wrong in the rebuilding.

She was lucky. Over there was the woman who'd lost a leg in a skiing accident; yesterday there had been a young man learning to use his left hand after his right one got crushed at work. All Kate had lost was ten months of her life. Not too bad, in the grand scheme of things.

Ten months of her life and ten months of Sam's life, too. Time she could never get back.

'Kate? Do you feel ready to try putting all your weight on both legs now?'

She refocused on Joseph. After a month of this, of seeing him every day, she thought she could read him pretty well.

'I'll try,' she said.

He smiled, his eyes lighting up. 'That's all we can do, Kate. Just try.'

She pulled herself upright, willing the feeling into her legs, giving them a little shake, summoning her resolve.

'And your core,' Joseph said. 'Remember your strength is in your core. Remember it gets easier every day.'

One step. That was all he wanted. Since the first time she'd been wheeled in here, still confused and groggy, all Joseph had wanted was one unaided step. He said that once she did that she would be able to carry on outside of their sessions, practising around the corridors of the hospital whenever she liked, and that before long she'd be running.

'I didn't run before,' she'd told him. 'Why would I want to now?'

Joseph had merely smiled that weary smile of his and said nothing.

One step. She pulled in her stomach, which felt hollow inside her loose clothing, and concentrated on visualising the blood flowing into her limbs; her muscles getting stronger; her bones the scaffolding that held her body together. She pushed off from the bars.

'Okay, now we're talking!' Joseph took a step back, but kept his eyes trained on hers. 'This is the day, Kate. I know it. You know how I get a feeling for these things. This is breakthrough day.'

She shook her head, smiling in spite of herself. Idiot.

'I want to do it just so I can get you to shut up with all the pep talks,' she said.

'Whatever floats your boat. Now stop talking and start moving.'

Her right foot was tingling, pins and needles starting up again, but her left foot felt okay. Better than okay – it felt almost normal. She shifted her weight slightly, then began to lift her left foot. One minute she could feel the mat under her toes, and then she couldn't feel it anymore.

'I think I'm doing it,' she said. Her voice rose in astonishment. Joseph said nothing.

Now there was an inch or more of space between the mat and her foot. Kate looked down to check. She wobbled.

'Look up,' Joseph commanded. 'Look at me.'

'Okay, but I ...'

It was too late. Kate began to wobble – at first a tremor snaking up from her tingling right leg, then a violent shaking all the way through her core. Lurching and clutching, her hands outstretched, Kate began to fall. She landed awkwardly, her elbow bent beneath her. When Joseph came to help her up she could barely see him through her tears.

'I'll never be able to do this,' she whispered.

'Yes, you will.' Joseph knelt on the floor and slid his hands around her waist, but she pushed him off and sat up by herself, drawing her knees into her chest. 'Kate, you can get around fine with the walker, and soon you'll be strong enough to walk with crutches.'

And then a stick, and then nothing. She knew all this. The theory was fine. It was all just taking too damn long. She shook her head, but couldn't speak. She thought about her son, trying to picture how he might look right now, what he might be doing. Was he thinking of her? Did he even know that she'd woken up?

Did he even know she'd been asleep?

'You will do this, Kate,' Joseph said again, 'but you won't do it for me, or for yourself.'

He stood and looked down at her. Kate could feel his eyes boring tunnels into her pain.

'You'll do it,' he said, 'for Sam.'

***

The letter arrived the following morning. For once, Kate wasn't waiting at her usual post, having hurt her hip along with her elbow when she fell the day before. She was still in bed, unable to face the idea of getting dressed yet, despite the cajoling of the shift-change nurses.

'Hey, good-looking.' The post boy's jaunty greeting didn't raise a smile, but when he held out an envelope – white with some large, looped writing on it – Kate practically leapt out of bed. She winced at the pain in her hip, then grabbed for the letter.

'Cornwall postcode and everything,' he said, grinning.

'Thanks,' Kate said, staring at the envelope. There was no mistaking those letter Es or that elaborate way of looping off the S.

She sat on her bed and ripped open the envelope. She read with her fingers in her mouth, chewing on her nails, biting down hard when she reached the end. So. At least she had her answer. Not that any of it made sense.

Kate shimmied to the edge of the bed, a sudden whirlwind of energy catching and containing her. She pulled all her things out of the fake wood cabinet and threw them on top of the crumpled covers; she scooped up spare underwear, her three books, her phone, her purse, all the items that had come with her onto the ward. The rest of her belongings from the flat had been packaged and put into storage before the flat was re-let – her landlord wasn't going to keep it empty for a woman who might never wake up, and clearly no one was willing to foot the bill on the off chance. She rammed everything that was on the bed into a pillowcase, tied a scruffy knot in the top, then yanked the curtain all the way back.

'Kate?' One of the nurses – one of the nice ones who didn't talk to her like she was three years old – came out from behind the nurses' station. 'Are we okay here?'

Kate didn't speak to her. She was dimly aware of the other people in the ward, of rows of beds and interested eyes. She reached for her walker. She could stand unaided now, and this gave her hope – she wouldn't be so helpless again. For now she needed this thing, but she wouldn't need it forever.

She began to move towards the ward's exit, her escape slower in reality than it had looked in her mind when she imagined it only moments ago, pulling her legs along by the force of her will alone.

'Kate,' the nurse said again. Her name was Bettina, or Letitia, Kate couldn't remember which. It didn't matter. All that mattered was getting to Sam.

She reached the double doors and slammed through them, turning instantly for the lift. From there the exit was only a stone's throw away. She would jump in a taxi, go to the train station; she would take a train from Manchester Piccadilly to St Austell; there would be one, even if it wasn't direct. Then another taxi to Corrin Cove. She hadn't been there since she was eighteen years old, but she could see it now as though she'd lived there only yesterday. Her parents' house. White-painted with roses around the door. Perfect in every way. Just like them.

Nothing like them.

'Kate.' A hand on her arm halted her progress. Someone took hold of her gently by her shoulders. She writhed out of their grip, but couldn't move far enough away to stop them getting hold of her again. When she looked up, angry, her face slick with sweat, she was surprised to see it was Joseph. Joseph and the nurse stood side by side, regarding her with expressions of such pity she wondered briefly what had happened.

'Can you just get out of my way?' she said, trying to edge the walker around them.

'Kate, where do you think you're going?' Joseph shooed the nurse away, turned back to Kate and began to walk alongside her.

'To see Sam, of course.' She didn't look at him. Keep your eyes on the prize, Kate. Joseph had told her this often enough during their sessions.

'Oh, right.' Joseph started to whistle. He was sauntering, his hands in the pockets of his tracksuit pants, while Kate huffed and puffed and struggled beside him. She was starting to tire. She had no intention of stopping.

'Don't try and stop me,' she warned him. 'This is a hospital, not a prison. I'm going to see my son like I should have weeks ago. Sitting around here, waiting for her to bring him to see me, when clearly she never had any intention of doing that. I've wasted so much time! Not anymore. My son needs me. Sam … Sam needs me.'

Her breath was coming in short bursts; she desperately wanted to sit down and take the crushing weight off her legs.

'I have to see him,' she said, throwing Joseph a challenging glare. 'I have to.'

'Sure. I know that.' Joseph looked at her – she could feel the intensity of his stare burn a hole in her cheek. Then he skipped ahead a couple of paces and took up a position ahead of her.

'Okay, Kate. We both know that you ain't going nowhere in this condition, with that thing slowing you down the whole time. Plus the fact that you've got no money, no proper clothing, and no real plan for this. So here's the deal.'

'You can keep your deal, Joseph,' Kate told him, panting. 'I'm going, and that's that.'

'Fine. Go as you are. You won't get out of the hospital. They need to discharge you first, and they won't do that until you're fit enough to look after yourself and have somewhere to actually go and live.'

He spread his legs into a wide, challenging stance. 'Here's what I will do, though. If you can walk from there to here, right now, I'll help you get out of here. I'll help you arrange your journey to Cornwall, I'll even lend you the money for your train fare. But only if you prove to me that you're ready to take that first step on your own.'

Joseph spoke softly; he was standing no more than four or five feet away from her, his hands hanging loosely at his sides. 'Do it, Kate. Think of Sam. If your mum won't bring him to see you, you'll have to go to him. And to do that, you need to get better. This is the only way.'

Kate looked down at her hands, the white knuckles gripping onto the walker, her wrists like pipe cleaners. She remembered how strong she'd felt when she gave birth to Sam, how vibrant, like the well of life sprang from her and her alone.

She swung the walking frame to one side and pushed it as hard as she could. It clattered away, smashing into the far side of the corridor with a satisfying echo. She tipped her chin into the air defiantly, then began to move forward. Her hands flew out to the sides for balance; her gait was uneven, half-shuffle, half-stagger. But she moved on her own, and Joseph held out his arms and caught her as soon as she was close enough. She expected a whoop of joy, a high-five or a cheer, but he just shrugged, then told her to stay where she was while he went to get her some crutches.

'I told you you could do it,' he said as he strolled away. 'You should have a little more faith in yourself, Kate.'

Chapter 2

'Kate?'

The woman who greeted her stood out in the crowd milling around in the station's concourse, not least because of her height. As Kate stepped forward with an uncertain tilt her to head, she wondered briefly what information Daniel, the social worker back in Manchester, had given to identify her. And then she laughed to herself. The crutch kind of gave it away.

'Did you have a good journey?' Elizabeth said. She was tall but well-built in a capable, stocky way. Daniel had said she seemed like just the kind of person to facilitate Kate's visit with Sam, and within moments Kate could see exactly why. Before Kate could even answer her first question, Elizabeth had whisked them into a waiting taxi, positioning Kate's crutch so that she could reach it easily and depositing her holdall on the floor by her feet. Kate felt as though her feet had hardly touched the floor – which was probably just as well: the new shoes she'd bought were absolute agony, but no way was she going to arrive at her parents' house wearing the shuffle-slippers she'd been living in for the past three months. She had some dignity left.

In the taxi, Elizabeth did exactly what Kate had hoped she would do: she filled Kate in on what had been happening this end from the perspective of social services. Kate sank back and listened, feeling like a real person again; like someone who was actually worth talking to.

'So, the first thing to bear in mind is that this is a sensitive situation,' Elizabeth said, pushing her sunglasses high on her head as she spoke. 'Your mother has been taking care of Sam now for over a year, and they've understandably become close. My feeling, Kate – and I'm telling you this in the strictest confidence – is the one and only reason she hasn't brought him to see you is that she's scared of losing him. Of course, there have been other reasons, all of them entirely plausible. So I could be one hundred percent wrong.'

'What are the reasons?' Kate asked, folding her hands over the bag on her lap and clasping them tightly.

'She wrote to you?' Elizabeth said.

'Yes.' Kate thought back to that letter. It still didn't make any sense. But then, nothing about the past year made any sense at all.

'Right. Well, there was an illness apparently – your father had been ill and so they couldn't travel. And then Sam had chicken pox–'

'Chicken pox! Poor baby! Was he okay? How bad was it?'

'He's fine, it's a common childhood disease.' Elizabeth pulled a notepad out of a smart leather briefcase and began to flick through it. Kate swallowed over a lump in her throat. Her little boy suffering from a childhood disease while she lay in a bed hundreds of miles away. How did he manage to get through it without his mother?

Not for the first time, she tried to imagine all the landmark moments she had missed. Had her mother recorded them for her? If there were photos, why hadn't she sent Kate any? Had she kept his first attempts at drawings, a lock of hair after his first haircut, the clothes he was wearing when Kate last saw him?

'Have you seen Sam?' she asked, clasping her hands

under her chin. 'Does he seem happy? Is he well?'

'He's a perfectly happy, well-adjusted little boy.' The social worker spoke without looking up. She was scribbling in her notepad, her handwriting spidery and indecipherable. Kate glanced out of the window but couldn't seem to focus her attention. Excitement was making her jittery – in a matter of minutes she would be seeing her son again, holding him, breathing in his scent. She had been waiting so long.

'Does he know who I am? Will he recognise me, do you think?'

Elizabeth shook her head. 'It's hard to say. And it depends on what your mother's told him to prepare for this visit.'

'A year isn't so very long, is it?' Kate mused, chewing on a nail. 'Well, not quite a full year. I mean, kids are resilient, aren't they? I was reading about it, one of the nurses lent me a book about child psychology. Sam will be fine. Won't he? He won't have been ... damaged by having me out of his life?'

'Your parents appear to have cared for him very well, Kate.'

She watched Elizabeth, absorbed in her notes again. 'You know, there's something that's been bothering me. And I think I need to get it off my chest.'

'Shoot,' Elizabeth said, leaning back and smiling. The taxi went over a bump and Kate's crutch clattered to the floor.

'Okay, I'm Sam's parent – not his only parent, obviously, but his dad has been out of the picture for a while.'

'Yes, so I understand.'

Kate glanced across at the social worker, who was still smiling impassively.

'Well, why didn't someone bring Sam to see his mother? Fine, you couldn't bring him right away, I understand that. I get it that the doctors were concerned for a while about brain damage, but I've been fine for weeks now. I mean, weeks and weeks. All I've been doing is waiting, waiting for Sam and waiting for my body to get strong enough to let me walk properly so I could leave the hospital. And ...'

She tailed off, aware that her voice was rising, her heart rate rising with it. 'I'd like,' she said shakily, 'to know why someone – you or Daniel or whoever had the authority – didn't simply collect Sam from my parents and bring him to see his mother. That's all.'

'Sure,' Elizabeth said briskly. 'Okay, well, the fact is, I guess we just didn't think it was necessary to pluck a nineteen-month-old child from the care of his grandparents, who clearly dote on him, and take him all the way to Manchester to be transferred to the care of someone who hadn't yet been discharged from hospital after a serious head injury and concussion – someone who was reported to be suffering from amnesia, couldn't care for herself independently, and didn't have anywhere to live. We considered that would not be in the best interests of the child.'

'Best interests ... Hold on, I'm his mother. This "someone" you keep talking about is his mother. What about my best interests? What about –'

'Kate.' Elizabeth held out her hands, palms together. Her tone was authoritative, although still gentle. 'With all due respect, this isn't about you. This is about Sam.'

Kate jerked her head away. She swallowed hard, surreptitiously wiping a tear from her cheek. 'I know,' she said, 'that this is about Sam. All I care about is Sam. It's just ... I've been so worried.'

'Well, then,' Elizabeth said, the matter-of-fact timbre firmly back in place, 'now we've got that out of the way, here's what I thought we'd do. We'll go and see Sam first – your parents are expecting us – and then I'll take you to your new lodgings. It's a nice house, right here in Corrin Cove. The landlady is a friend of my sister. There are two rooms, one for you and one for Sam. It'll be perfectly adequate until we get you sorted with something more permanent.'

'Is it furnished?' Kate said, trying to imagine the sheer scale of what she had to do to make a home now for herself and her son.

'It is. We thought Sam could come for visits first, maybe stay overnight, and you can get to know what kinds of toys he likes, what kinds of things he's into.'

Kate looked at the woman in astonishment. 'Come for visits? He won't need to visit me, he'll be living with me.' A hole began to form inside Kate's stomach, an empty, nervous space that sensed only the worst. 'Are you saying he won't be coming home with me today? Is that what you're saying?'

Elizabeth said nothing. Kate wondered what her mother had told this woman about her wayward daughter. It was true she'd found it hard to cope with Sam when he was tiny and colicky, and all those nights without sleep had worn her down, making her feel as though she was disappearing into a maelstrom of confusion. How her mother had loved being superior then, when Kate had called out of the blue and asked for help. How she'd gloated.

The taxi driver slid back his privacy panel and called out for directions.

'It's just down there,' Elizabeth instructed, pointing to a narrow track, part hidden by a yew hedge. She bent to pick up Kate's crutch, a sheet of fair hair hiding her impenetrable face. Before Kate could ask any more questions, the social worker was out of the taxi and standing on the kerb, hunting in her purse for change.

Kate gripped her crutch and looked out of the window, out into another time. Woodland Cottage sat on the outskirts of the seaside town of Corrin Cove, its white-rendered walls and grey slate roof stark against the year-round emerald lawns and trees. Kate had spent her childhood here, playing in the woods behind the house, building dens and tree houses, places to escape to. When she left, she had vowed never to return.

'Okay,' Elizabeth said, hoisting Kate's bag onto her shoulder. 'Are you ready to see your son?'

Chapter 3

He was an angel. An angel in short blue trousers and a Postman Pat T-shirt. Kate gazed at him, drinking him in, unable to take her eyes off him for a second. She had expected to feel more pain than this, to feel the full weight of everything she'd missed out on, but right now all she felt was joy. Pure, beautiful joy.

Kate sat on the floor, leaning over her son as far as she could, drinking in his scent. The sun streaked through the glass, lighting up his thick blonde hair, his scalp covered completely now, his head round and solid. He was sitting upright, chunky legs stuck out to the sides, stacking cups. 'That one,' he said, pointing with a chubby finger to the next in the sequence. Kate passed him the yellow cup wordlessly. It was, she realised with a jolt, the first time she'd ever heard him speak.

His face showed an almost comical expression of concentration as he placed the cup on top of the stack, then he looked up in delight, grinning, waiting for approval.

'Oh, well done!' exclaimed Kate. 'Well done.'

She caught her breath. She was having a conversation with her son. It was almost too momentous to take in.

His hair was cut short, close to his head, but instead of making him look a little thuggish, like it could on some boys his age, on Sam it was angelic. He gave off a solid, contented aura, impossible to describe, and all Kate wanted was to pick him up again and crush him to her chest, as she had the second he'd toddled into the room, clutching his grandmother's hand at the sight of two strangers. That was what her mother had called her. A stranger.

'You'll frighten him,' Barbara had said, her arms folded, watching Kate and Sam through wary eyes. 'Give him a bit of space. He's not good with strangers.'

'Kate's hardly a stranger.' Elizabeth's gentle rebuke had fallen on deaf ears. Barbara stayed on the edges of the sun room; Kate's father was nowhere to be seen.

Sam was murmuring under his breath now, and he pushed the stacking cups over, reaching instead for a box of brightly coloured bricks. 'Need blue ones,' he insisted solemnly, gazing up at Kate. She nodded, awestruck.

'He speaks really well,' she said, glancing up at her mother. 'For his age, I mean.'

Barbara shrugged. 'You did too, at that age.'

'When did he ...' Kate didn't know where to start. When did he walk, run, climb, eat his first ice cream, fall over for the first time?

Has he had all his jabs and vaccinations, is he healthy, does he ever have nightmares ...?

Does he ever ask about me?

Her unspoken questions hung in the air. Elizabeth coughed and pulled her notebook out of her briefcase again. She turned to a page with a yellow sticky note attached to the top.

'Mrs Steiner,' she said, 'I think Kate has a few questions for you, and it might be an idea for her to ask them while I'm here.'

Kate wondered who Elizabeth was trying to protect: her or her mother. Then she realised that the social worker didn't care a jot about either of them. She was only interested in Sam.

'I'd like to know why you didn't visit me in the hospital,' Kate said softly. Sam regarded her with clear, calm eyes. Kate smiled at him, trying to send him all the love she had in her heart. He turned away, disinterested.

There was a pause, then Elizabeth spoke up. 'Kate would like to know why you didn't go and –'

'I heard her,' Barbara interrupted. 'There's no need for her to talk to the floor like a child.'

'Maybe you could just tell her,' Elizabeth suggested. 'Explain your reasons. I'm sure Kate will understand once she hears them in your own words.'

Kate rolled a ball along the floor to Sam, wishing the two of them could go somewhere else and be alone together.

'Well, I did come,' Barbara said. 'David and I came every day for the first few weeks. We had no idea what would happen, to Kate or to Samuel. We visited her in the hospital – I brought her some things from the flat, and we brought Samuel to see her.'

'And then,' Elizabeth prompted.

'The doctors told us it was very unlikely she'd wake up from the coma. They said she might be brain damaged, or worse. We were looking after Sam with us in a hotel, but it wasn't ideal. So we made the decision to come back here. It was for the best.' Barbara voice rose with a hint of defensiveness that made Kate look up from the floor. Her mother was talking to Elizabeth; it was as though Kate didn't exist. Kate bit her lip, taking her attention away from Sam with extreme reluctance.

'But when you heard that I had woken up, when you found out I was going to be alright, why didn't you visit again then? You could have phoned or written. Weren't you happy to hear that I was okay?'

'Of course I was.' For a moment, Kate saw a flash of pain cross her mother's face, but seconds later it was gone. 'It was hard for us, seeing you lying there in the hospital. You can't imagine. I'm glad – more than glad – to see you so recovered now, to see you well again.'

Barbara's gaze slid to Kate's crutch, which was propped up against the side of the sofa, then she turned to face Elizabeth. 'Kate and her father and I had been estranged for many years,' she explained. 'I had seen Kate briefly when Sam was three months old, but prior to that we'd had no relationship for a long time. I had reconciled myself to the fact that our daughter did not want us in her life.'

'Briefly?' Kate echoed in astonishment. 'Mum, you came and stayed with Sam and me for over a month. You fed him at night, changed him, took him out in his pram. We had ... we had meals together, walks together. I thought it was okay between us, I thought –'

'Which was exactly why,' Barbara continued, once again addressing Elizabeth, 'it seemed appropriate for David and I to look after the boy when his mother was no longer able to.'

'I see.' Elizabeth paused, then wrote something in her notebook. She glanced up and looked directly at Kate. There was something in her expression Kate didn't like at all. She couldn't be sure, but she thought it was pity.

'Mrs Steiner,' Elizabeth said, 'perhaps you would like to explain to your daughter the steps you took to safeguard Sam's future.' Her tone was wary, guarded. Kate looked at her mother in surprise.

'What steps?' A small hand touched her leg, and she glanced down and saw her son trying to climb onto her lap. She reached for him and he came readily, fitting into her arms, still holding two of his bricks in chubby fingers.

'Blue,' he said. Kate smiled and kissed his head.

'Yes,' she told him. 'Blue. Very good.'

Barbara was watching them, her expression unreadable. Kate could sense that the atmosphere between them was beginning to make even Elizabeth uncomfortable, although Kate imagined the woman had been in far worse situations than this. She smiled to herself grimly. Welcome to a Steiner family reunion. We all love each other here.

Taking strength from her son's tacit approval, Kate decided to do her best to see things from her mother's point of view. She had done well by Sam; she only had his best interests at heart. There was a long way to go, there were still many questions to answer, but today was not the day to air old grievances.

'What steps have you taken, Mum?' Kate asked again, but this time she smiled warmly, hugging Sam to her chest.

Her mother registered the tiniest sign of discomfort. She smoothed her hands down the sides of her immaculately cut skirt, and crossed her trim ankles neatly.

'As I said earlier, we – your father and I – were under the impression you very likely would not wake up from the coma, or indeed recover from the injuries you sustained. Therefore, we decided after having Sam with us for six months that we would make it official.'

'Official?' Kate held Sam tight against her body. He fitted the bricks together, then unclamped them. Together, apart. He giggled, then held them up to show to Kate. She kissed his cheek, never taking her eyes from her mother's face.

'Official, yes. So that he would be protected.' As Barbara spoke, she finally met Kate's gaze. Her eyes were cold, her expression unflinching.

Kate felt a chill settle over her, prickling her scalp, raising goose bumps on her arms. The warmth from Sam's little body did nothing to counter it. He began to wriggle, good-naturedly pushing himself out of her arms before toddling away with a wide-legged gait to the toy box across the room. Kate sat on the cold tiles and stared up at the two women who looked down at her, one full of sympathy, the other a study in antipathy. Her leg had gone to sleep, and now she was unable to reach her crutch or find the strength to push herself up from the floor.

Elizabeth spoke softly. 'Your parents applied for Special Guardianship, Kate. The court awarded it three months ago. They have parental responsibility for Sam now, too. I'm sorry. I should have told you sooner. I thought–' she paused and glanced at Barbara, whose expression was still carved from stone. 'I thought it might have been better for your mother to explain it. It seems I was quite wrong.'

'But who,' said Kate, her voice rasping in her throat, 'who did you need to protect him from?'

Yet even as she said the words, she knew. Her mother's letter, the oblique references to Kate's lifestyle and background, the tone of judgment, as though Kate herself were responsible for the attack, the coma, everything. She knew. Her parents were trying to protect Sam from his own mother.

And if that were the case, there must be a reason.

Just how much else had her amnesia made her forget?

***

They sat on the promenade, on a concrete bench, with seagulls shouting and squawking around them. The sound of children playing in the breakers on the shoreline was almost too much for Kate to bear. And yet at the same time it was comforting. Elizabeth sat silently by her side, thumbing through her phone, occasionally tapping out a message, or writing something in her notepad. The sun was relentless; it was an all-or-nothing kind of summer this year. Kate had been protected in hospital, only going outside into the atrium once a day for fresh air. Here, exposed to the sea air and the brash

August climate in Corrin Cove, Kate felt more vulnerable than ever.

'They found drugs in your flat,' Elizabeth said with a sigh. 'It was in the police report. To be honest, I thought you knew. After you'd gone in the ambulance, the police dusted for prints, tried to work out if anything had been taken, the usual stuff. They found evidence of drug use, and a large quantity of cannabis. Plenty of people take recreational drugs, Kate. But I guess your parents ... Well, they're obviously kind of judgmental.'

Kate shook her head, incredulous. 'But – I don't take drugs. I mean, I did, once. A long time ago. It was Evan, Sam's dad. He lived that kind of lifestyle, not me, although I guess I did get drawn into it at one time. I'm not making excuses but ... I hadn't taken anything for months before I got pregnant with Sam, Elizabeth, and certainly not after! For goodness sake, what do you take me for?'

Elizabeth shrugged. 'It's no skin off my nose what you did. Like I said, I'm just here to make sure Sam's okay.'

'So you think I was a bad parent too, is that it? That's clearly what my mother thinks, and that's why she's done this. It all makes sense now, doesn't it?'

The relentless questions of the policewoman who visited her in hospital, who, now Kate came to think about it, had always had a noticeable edge of suspicion and disapproval in her face. Daniel's reluctance to share information with her; the vagueness of the doctors and the rest of the staff; her mother's letter – the coldness in her eyes. They all thought she was a druggie. It was completely, entirely crazy.

'And what, they think that was what the attack was about? A drug deal gone wrong?'

Elizabeth looked out towards the horizon. Her sunglasses were no longer holding back her hair, and Kate couldn't see her eyes. 'Something like that.'

'They basically think I brought this on myself?'

'I can't tell you what the police think, Kate. And I probably shouldn't be discussing with you what was in the report they released to us. But they didn't press charges, so they can't have thought your involvement overtly criminal.'

'My involvement? I was hit over the head and knocked unconscious! I was unconscious for nearly ten months. How could they have pressed charges when I was in a coma?'

Elizabeth gave a sound that was halfway between a sigh and a laugh. 'My dear, I've seen cases where the police have arrested someone within minutes of them coming round after a car crash where the rest of their family died. You don't know the half of it.'

Kate decided she didn't want to. She clasped her hands together and turned to face Elizabeth, blinking against a sudden burst of sea air that brought the taste of sand to her lips.

'Listen. I don't care what they think. I know the truth, and I'm telling you now that I never touched drugs, or even took one single alcoholic drink, all the time I was caring for Sam. My father is an alcoholic, did you know that? He's a hypocrite, and she protects him – neither one of them is fit to look after my son, I don't care what your special order says. But I'm here on my own now, I have no one, no family, no friends, just a boy who doesn't even know who I am. If I'm going to get through this I need to know that at least one person believes the truth. Do you think you could be that person?'

Elizabeth reached up and took off her sunglasses. Her eyes were green in the slanted light, and measuring. She regarded Kate for a second or two, then she replaced the glasses and looked back out to sea. 'Sure,' she said. 'I believe you. No problem.'

Chapter 4

Barbara Steiner took a glass jar down from the top shelf and removed two tea bags from it. These she flung into the waiting cups, tapping her nails on the shiny worktop while the kettle boiled ferociously. Her husband stood three feet behind her. She could sense him although he'd yet to speak.

The argument had started, like they so often seemed to these days, during breakfast. She knew it was partly her fault – waiting until this morning to tell him about their daughter's visit had been unfair. He had reacted exactly as she'd predicted, proving she'd been right not to tell him any earlier.

'I should have been here,' he had thundered, throwing his paper down onto the polished table as he pushed himself to his feet. 'I can't believe you arranged it all behind my back.'

'It wasn't intentional,' Barbara had countered. 'She came with that social worker – I didn't have much say over the date. And you always play golf on Fridays. I didn't think you'd want your routine to be disrupted.'

He stood behind her now, but Barbara didn't turn around. Let him be the first one to speak. It had been a long time since he'd lost his temper like that. So long she'd almost forgotten. The kettle clicked off. She poured water into the cups, then stood and watched the teabags steeping, not wanting to cross the kitchen to get the milk, not wanting to move past her husband.

'You know, I hardly recognised her yesterday,' Barbara said. 'I thought about the girl we raised, that sweet little girl, and then I thought about the last time we saw her, lying in hospital, dead to the world.'

'I want to see her.' David was standing closer now; she could feel his breath on her neck. 'There are things I need to say.'

Barbara closed her eyes. 'You realise that she wants to take Samuel away from us, don't you? That's what she's here for, David. That's all she's here for. She hasn't come to make things right, to say sorry for all the lies she told about you the day she left home. There were no signs of remorse, or regret, or sadness. Not for us, anyway.'

She turned to him. His skin was mottled red, with white patches around his mouth. Anger. Or something else. She hoped it was anger.

'You do remember, don't you?' she pressed. 'You remember the lies she told? How much she hurt you? Hurt us?'

'Stop it. I don't want to rake over old ground anymore. The next time Kate visits, I want to be here. Understand?' He picked up his cup and poured the contents into the sink. Then he grabbed his keys from the counter and headed for the door.

'David – wait.' She half ran after him, catching his sleeve as he pulled on his jacket. 'Where are you going?'

'Out.'

'She won't want to see you. She hates you.'

Her hand flew up to her mouth involuntarily, and she took a step away from him. But David only regarded her sadly.

'I know what you're thinking,' he said, 'but it won't work.'

She squared her shoulders. 'What am I thinking?'

'Barbara, you brought the boy here, it was your decision and I supported you in it. But now our daughter

24

is well again and she is here, on our own doorstep, and you can't ... You should give Sam back to her, Barbara. Like you said, he's her son.'

'Give him back? Are you mad?' Barbara paled. She steadied herself against a console table. 'What are you saying?'

'I'm saying that we were only ever looking after him until she got better, and now she's better.'

'He's not a toy we borrowed, David! He's a little boy.' Her voice was edging close to hysteria; her husband stopped her with a frown, but then he swallowed and looked away. She noticed his eyes, the pinkness around them. Wavery, not quite focused. She should stop him driving, but she knew from experience it would only lead to another row. She didn't have the energy for another row.

Barbara glared at her husband's departing back with something close to hatred. Give Samuel back to Kate? How could he even suggest such a thing? She closed the door softly behind him, then held her hands over her eyes to cool them. No matter what happened, whatever her daughter said or did – whatever David said or did – no one would take Samuel away from her. She simply could not let that happen.

***

The woman was twenty minutes late. It simply wasn't good enough, not when the appointment had been arranged for a specific time, and Barbara had had to arrange for a babysitter for Samuel. It was hot and sticky in the waiting room, but Barbara had worn her lightest linen shift dress, and had twisted her hair into a French pleat so it didn't lie heavily on her neck. She tapped her fingers on the arm of the wooden chair. Was it so very difficult to keep to an appointment system? She supposed solicitors were very busy and important and constantly in demand, dealing as they must with all sorts of undesirables.

Her last visit had been no different. This was where she had sought advice six months ago, found out about the Special Guardianship Order. At least then they'd offered her a cup of tea. Today, nothing. She glanced at the collection of dog-eared magazines again. Pseudo celebrity gossip and "real life" stories to make your toes curl. No, thank you very much.

Finally her name was called and she walked through the double doors into Bridget Cohen's office. This was more like it – wooden panelling, certificates on the walls, a nice view of the bay. The prosperity of her legal counsel calmed her: she was in safe hands now.

'Mrs Steiner. How nice to see you again.'

Barbara sat down and shook her solicitor's hand.

Bridget flicked through a manila file on her desk, then pulled out a sheet of paper and gave it a cursory glance. 'Here we are. Samuel Steiner. And how is Samuel doing?'

Barbara hadn't come all this way to indulge in small talk. 'As I said on the phone, my daughter, Samuel's mother, has ... Well, she has recovered from her accident and appears to be quite fit and well, and now she wants to take her son back.' Barbara paused and smoothed her palms along the length of her thighs. 'I told her that we have an order from the court to look after the boy, so she can't simply take him away. That is correct, is it not?'

The solicitor regarded Barbara steadily. 'May I ask you a question, Mrs Steiner?'

Barbara nodded.

'Why don't you want Samuel to be with his natural mother?'

It was a simple enough question, but one Barbara was not prepared for. She stared at Bridget in alarm.

'Why would you ask me that? We can provide a loving, stable home for him, which is exactly what he needs. He's a happy boy, healthy and full of life. And what does it say in that file of yours? You were the one who showed me the police report. Kate was a drug addict before Samuel was born, and what they found in her flat proved that she'd gone back to her old habits. Do you think I'm just going to hand him over and say, "There you go, have a nice life"? We haven't been looking after the boy for the weekend – it's been almost a year!'

'Presumably she has missed her son rather a lot in that case,' Bridget said, clearly nonplussed by Barbara's outburst. She closed the file and threaded her hands together. 'Mrs Steiner, do you any have reason to suspect that your daughter is still involved with her former habits now, today?'

What an unusual way to put it. Barbara shrugged. How could she know for sure? She felt her face heating up as she realised she hadn't even considered where Kate might be staying in Corrin Cove, or who she might be staying with. Probably that frightful social worker thought Barbara was the worst kind of mother possible for not welcoming her daughter into her home with open arms.

'If your daughter decides to apply for a variation of the order, the case will go to court,' Bridget continued. 'In the majority of these cases, the court will naturally consider that a child's rightful place is with its mother. It would be up to any interested party to prove otherwise, but the proof would have to be compelling.'

Barbara digested these words. She couldn't help noticing that the other woman's nails were bitten and the varnish chipped. This somewhat diminished the authority of the wooden panelling and the framed certificates on the walls.

'So what you're saying is, I must prove that my daughter is an unfit mother? That it would be dangerous to let her have Samuel back?'

Bridget frowned and shook her head. 'No, Mrs Steiner, I'm not suggesting that at all, and I am not advising that as a course of action. It would be incredibly painful for all involved, I'm sure. How could you and your daughter have a relationship after that? Samuel must lose either his mother or his grandparents. Defending a contested guardianship order is not a decision to be taken lightly. My advice is that you come to terms with her amicably, maybe share Samuel's care for a while, until she gets back on her feet. '

'Thank you for your advice,' Barbara said stiffly. 'But what I want are facts. Can we keep Samuel or not?'

The solicitor sighed. 'You can try,' she said. 'But unless you have a very good reason for believing Samuel would be unsafe with his own mother, I strongly advise against it.'

Barbara felt her jaw tightening. Come to terms? After everything Kate had said and done? After the risks her daughter had taken with Samuel's health and wellbeing? She just couldn't imagine how she could ever trust her again.

'My advice, which is what you're paying for, after all,' Bridget said tiredly, 'is to make it up with your daughter. That way she will still let you and your husband see Samuel so you won't lose him completely. Don't make an enemy of her, Mrs Steiner. In my experience, it just isn't worth it.'

Barbara stepped out of the building into the bright sunlight and groped around in her bag for her sunglasses, realising with annoyance that she had left them at home. A group of teenagers pushed passed her, forcing her into the wall, and she opened her mouth to shout after them but closed it again quickly. Instead she made her way back to the car park where she sank into the safely of her pristine Nissan with a sigh of relief. Big towns made her nervous. She preferred to be at home, listening to Samuel chatting away while he played on the floor or at the kitchen table, watching the birds in the garden, just feeling time settle upon her like a blanket. Sometimes he was the only person she would see for days; David was out more often now he had retired than he had been when he worked.

Without the boy she'd have no one.

She started the engine and turned on the stereo. A nursery rhyme, volume set to deafening, blared out of the speakers. Barbara smiled and tipped back her head. She looked at the rear-view mirror, picturing Samuel's cherubic little face gazing back at her, singing along to the words they both knew by heart. She missed his solid, brightening presence even when she had to pop into town without him, or while he took a nap in the daytime.

How could she survive a day without him permanently in her life?

She knew what she had to do. The meeting with the solicitor had not been entirely wasted. This was a game of wit and nerve, and she still had a couple of cards to play.

Chapter 5

The house was near the end of a long narrow street that climbed its way up from the promenade to the crest of Bow Hill. It was a house Kate had walked past many times during her early teenage years, hanging out with friends on the corner by the off-licence where Bow Hill met the Parade – a strip of down-at-heel shops offering bric-a-brac and sun hats and dubious grocery items to any intrepid holidaymakers who happened to make it up this far from the sea. The Parade was still there; Kate had walked to it for the past two mornings to buy rolls for breakfast, a tin of soup for lunch.

Marie, her landlady, came out to greet her as soon as Kate stepped in off the street. Kate imagined Marie waiting behind the door that led to her own private part of the house, listening, anticipating, gathering up her energy. She seemed to have no life or occupation of her own, seemed happy to spend hours trailing after Kate, chatting on in that inexhaustible way she had, her life story an open book. After only two days, Kate knew that Marie was divorced – bitterly, regretfully divorced – from a man she was now once again dating; she knew that Marie and her ex, known as Big Tony to his friends, had no children together, but that Tony had sired two boys with two different women during breaks from Marie. The exact nature of these breaks was constantly up for examination and negotiation, and seemed to be the source of most of their conflict: Tony maintaining that he had been free to do whatever he wished with whomever he liked; Marie convinced that she was under the impression they were still in fact together during many of his flings.

It was exhausting, but Kate didn't mind. While Marie held forth, Kate could take herself out of her own mind, albeit briefly, and the pain dulled just a little.

But it never went away for long.

After Elizabeth had brought her here on Friday, Kate had sat in the room set aside for Sam and tried to conjure him back into her reality. The feel of his hair against her cheek; the smoothness of his skin. She had pictured him playing on the bobbly brown carpet, and sketched out his face on the back of her train ticket. She'd lain flat on her back and gazed at the ceiling until her eyes blurred.

Elizabeth had promised to be in touch soon to arrange Kate's next visit with Sam. All weekend she had paced and fretted, desperate to go back to Woodland Cottage. Kate had no intention of staying away. She hadn't come all this way to sit around and wait. Her main problem was how to get there. It was too far to walk – maybe not for an able-bodied person, but for Kate with her crutch it was out of the question. She had arrived in Corrin Cove with a small amount of cash – her bank balance, dormant for a year, told the story of how badly she'd been struggling before the break-in. When she finally located the number of a local taxi service, she was dismayed at the cost of even such a short journey. No matter. Seeing Sam was all that counted.

'Kate, you're up and about early,' Marie said, wafting into the hall as Kate closed the front door behind her. 'Any news yet?'

Of course, when someone confides in you so easily, there's no way to hold back with your own story.

Kate shook her head. 'I'm going over there today,

regardless. I don't care what anyone says.'

'Quite right,' Marie said briskly, slipping her hand under Kate's elbow and walking her towards the narrow staircase that led to Kate's rooms on the first floor, and another on the second. 'Would you like me to come with you? A bit of moral support?'

'Oh, no thank you,' Kate said, alarmed. The thought of Marie, exotic with her hippy-style tunics and oversized wooden jewellery and dyed-black lacquered hair, sitting in her mother's pristine, stuffy sun room filled her with dread. But then she felt guilty. Marie had shown her more care and humanity in two days than her mother had in thirty years. Still, Kate couldn't imagine the two of them together, breathing the same air. She gave Marie's hand a squeeze. 'It's sweet of you to offer, but this is something I need to do on my own.'

'Of course you do.' Marie released Kate on the first floor landing, holding on to the balustrade as though she might fall over without it. 'Would you like me to ask Patrick to give you a lift? I'm sure he'd be happy to.' Marie lowered her voice, her eyes trained on the ceiling. 'I happen to know he's a bit low this week. I think he might have a birthday looming.' She grinned at Kate conspiratorially. 'I'm going to bake him a cake.'

This seemed to be typical of Marie, Kate thought. Never mind that her other lodger might not want a fuss made, she would bake a cake regardless and downright make sure he enjoyed himself.

'Have you met our Patrick yet?' Marie asked, grinning. 'He's rather a dish.'

Kate shook her head. 'I'd better go, I–'

'I could introduce you now if you like, I know he's in. And I'm sure he'd be happy to give you a lift,' Marie added, heading for the second floor.

'Really, I wouldn't want to bother him. Or you,' Kate added with another weak smile, turning quickly to unlock her room.

Once inside she laid her crutch on the floor and leaned against the door, listening for the sound of Marie's footsteps on the stairs. There was a pause, twenty seconds, no more, and then Marie began to descend, singing a pop song Kate didn't recognise. A year of pop songs, news reports, movie releases and all kinds of trivia that were lost to her now. She hadn't the time, or the inclination, to try and catch up.

It would be nice, Kate thought as she crossed the room, to have a friend like Marie. She imagined Marie to be the kind of friend who would keep you sane, even as she drove you crazy from time to time.

Her phone rang, loud and insistent. It was Elizabeth.

'Kate, how are things going there?'

Straight in, no small talk. Kate liked that about her. 'The rooms are fine,' she said. 'Except one of them is missing a small boy.'

'Right.' Elizabeth paused. Kate could hear other voices in the background; she pictured Elizabeth in a vast open space, with phones ringing, desks rammed together, lots of activity. Her offices were in St Austell, the main town just up the coast. 'So, I spoke to your mother this morning. We've arranged another visit for Wednesday, two o'clock. Do you want me to come and pick you up or shall we meet there?'

'Wednesday?' Kate couldn't keep the disappointment from her voice. 'You're kidding, right? I'm not waiting until Wednesday. That's almost a week. Elizabeth, I miss my baby so much. I want to take care of him, to be there for him.'

'I know, Kate.' Elizabeth's voice became muffled, as though she'd put her hand over the phone. Then she spoke again. 'I'm posting the forms out to you today – you'll need to sign them and get them back to me as soon as you can.'

Kate nodded. An application to discharge the Special Guardianship Order. It sounded so official. 'I'll do that, don't worry. But I'm not waiting until Wednesday to see Sam, Elizabeth. I just can't do it.'

'I thought you might say that. Kate, these people are your family – there's nothing to stop you visiting them whenever you want to.'

'And Sam is my son.'

'Exactly. Just ... go easy, okay? Believe me, cases like this that go to family court, things can very easily get out of hand.'

They talked about the arrangements Kate had made for her things to be sent down from Manchester, then Elizabeth said she had to go.

'I'll see you on Wednesday. Just try to hang on until then.'

Easy for her to say. 'Elizabeth, can I just ask you one more thing? What reasons did my mother give for making me wait until Wednesday?'

Elizabeth sighed, impatient now. 'She just said they were busy, they had plans. She said she'd promised him a trip to the beach.'

'Well, I could meet them at the beach,' Kate suggested, but Elizabeth was already saying goodbye.

Her mother had always accused her of being wilful, Kate thought as she stomped onto the landing ten minutes later. She was probably right. But wilful had its uses, and determination had certainly helped Kate get back on her feet faster than most people when her muscles were wasted and her body weak. She thrust her crutch out purposefully – right into the path of a tall man who was just that moment rounding the bottom of the stairs to the second floor.

'Oh, my ... I'm so sorry,' Kate said, her face already burning with embarrassment. The man shook his head and smiled, then bent to pick up her crutch. She registered broad shoulders, a strong back, casual clothes in muted colours, and thick brown hair that curled slightly over his ears.

'No worries,' told her. She noticed that his brown eyes were shaped like almonds, crinkling in at the corners. He smelt of the outdoors, of forests and the wide sky and summers spent digging around in the bare earth. Kate inhaled, momentarily lost.

'Do you want this back?' he asked her. He was holding out the crutch, still smiling.

'Oh, yes. Of course. I only need it because I, erm, I had an accident. I hardly need it at all, really, to be honest.'

'Did you break your leg or something?' he enquired, glancing down at her legs.

Kate reddened, suddenly aware of her unfashionable shorts showing too much pale skin and of her worn-down, grubby sandals. 'No. I was ...' She swallowed and hoisted her bag higher over her shoulder. 'It's kind of complicated.'

'Okay.' He nodded, then held out his hand. 'I'm Patrick. I live on the floor above.'

'Kate,' she said, shaking his hand. His palm was warm and dry, and the contact sent a jolt of heat through her forearm.

'Nice to meet you, Kate,' he said softly. 'See you around, I'm sure.'

'I hope so,' Kate whispered as he carried on down the stairs. She knew he hadn't heard her, but when she turned to follow him, she found herself holding onto the balustrade for support, just as Marie had done earlier.

Chapter 6

They were easy to spot. Kate's mother stood out from the others on the beach: not a pre-school mummy or a holiday maker; not a groovy granny or childminder or an office worker on a lunchtime break. Alongside the young mums with their toddlers and buckets and spades and picnics and brightly coloured beach towels she looked old and careworn, despite the expensive clothes and the perfectly styled hair. Or maybe because of it.

Kate picked her way across the sand towards them, trying to arrange her face into a surprised expression. Her mother had set up camp with a large parasol for Sam to play under, while she herself sat on a fold-out chair, reading a book, her back straight, ankles crossed. Sam looked adorable in a pink sun hat, and Kate had to bite her lip to stop herself from shouting out to him from all the way across the promenade.

As soon as she was close enough to have noticed them naturally, she began to wave.

'Hey, there,' she called brightly. 'What a coincidence!'

Sam looked up from his sandcastle, squinting in the harsh light. She reached his side and squatted down beside him.

'Hi, Sam, how are you? I've missed you. What are you building?' She planted a quick kiss on his cheek. He tasted of sun cream and his skin was gritty with sand. Kate looked up at her mother and smiled, shielding her eyes with her hand. 'Hello, Mum.'

Her mother marked her place in the book with her finger. She said, 'What are you doing here, Kate?'

'Well, I'm just enjoying the sunshine, same as you.'

Sam offered Kate a bucket half-filled with shells; she took it and kissed the top of his head.

'Did Elizabeth tell you we'd be here?' Barbara said.

Kate inspected her bitten-down nails. 'Yes. Okay, she did. And I came looking for you. But it's a free country. I'm just enjoying half an hour on the beach with my son and my mother. I'm not doing any harm.'

Barbara said nothing. The sounds of the seaside settled over them – seagulls screeching and children squealing, the waves breaking on the shore. Sam's chatter soothed Kate's mind, and soon she relaxed, stretching out her legs in the sand, laughing when Sam decided to try and bury her feet. She wriggled her toes, tipping back her long hair, feeling the heat of the sun on her bare shoulders.

Barbara unpacked a picnic, and Kate watched, fascinated, as Sam drink a beaker of milk and ate his sandwiches. The last time she'd seen him eat she had been spooning him mashed-up sweet potato and milk mixed with baby rice. Now he was sitting up unaided, feeding himself with his own sticky fingers.

'Mum,' she began, as Barbara cleaned Sam's face with a wipe and started to tidy away their lunch things, 'I just want to say–'

'We have to get back,' Barbara interrupted. 'Sam has a nap in the afternoon. He gets very tired otherwise.'

'No, Nana,' Sam wailed, stamping his foot in the sand. 'No nap.'

'Sam.' Kate kneeled next to her son and wrapped him in her arms. 'You must do as your Nana says. Sleep is important. I should know,' she added, smiling ruefully at her mother. 'I was asleep for almost a year.'

But Barbara didn't return her smile. 'Thank you,' she

said stiffly. 'Sam, pick up your bucket now and let's go.'

Sam shook his head. 'No,' he told her. He sat down on his bottom suddenly, covering himself in sand all over again. 'Not coming. No nap.' He pointed to Kate, who was fitting her crutch back under her arm in preparation for the trek along the beach. 'Only if she come too.'

***

Being allowed to go back to the house with them might have seemed like a minor victory – and given Kate precious opportunities for extra cuddles, and the chance to observe his new toddler-size car seat arrangement – but all too soon Sam was whisked away and taken upstairs for his nap. Kate waited at the bottom of the stairs. There was something she needed to know before she left.

'Mum,' she said, when Barbara descended holding a baby monitor to her ear, 'where's Dad? Why wasn't he here on Friday?'

'He was busy.' Barbara glided past her and moved into the kitchen. Kate waited a beat, then followed.

'That's it? Too busy to see his own daughter? Tell me the truth – he doesn't want to see me, does he? He's still too angry. Or is it that he can't face me?'

She watched her mother grip the edge of the sink, saw her shoulders raise, then lower.

'Yes, Kate. You're right. He is still very angry. That's why I've arranged your visits with Sam for days when he isn't here. To protect you. I thought ... I thought it would be for the best.'

'Oh. Well, okay. And ... how are things with him?'

Her mother crossed the room and folded herself into a chair. She smoothed her skirt, then laid her hands on her lap. 'I don't know what you mean,' she said.

Kate positioned her crutch at her elbow, suddenly

feeling at a disadvantage standing as she was in front of the window while her mother sat serenely at the table in the shade. She began to move out of the sun, but was stopped in her tracks by her mother's words.

'I see you have a new crutch to lean on, Kate. No need for the drugs anymore?'

Kate rocked back, her face burning. 'That's uncalled for, and you know it. I wasn't taking drugs, Mum, and I have no idea how they got into my flat. Sam and I were making a new life for ourselves, away from all that. Away from Evan and his poison. And you were a part of that new life. I thought we were making progress when you came to stay.'

'I left your father on his own here,' Barbara said. 'He was sick, he begged me not to come. He said he'd never forgive me, but I still came. I wanted to be there for you, for my daughter. And my grandson.'

'Well, I didn't know that. You never said he was ill. But you know I was grateful. You got me – you got us – through a bad patch.'

'You couldn't cope with a baby,' Barbara snapped. 'It was obvious to me you were making a complete mess of it.'

Kate tried to calm herself. She took another shaky breath.

'Look, I am so grateful for the way you've looked after Sam. I can see how happy he is, what a great job you've done.'

'It isn't a job, he's my responsibility. I have a court order that says so.'

'Right. And to be honest, I'm surprised you're not waving it in front of my face right now. Mum, that court order won't mean a thing when they find out Sam's own mother is perfectly fit and well and is living right here in Corrin Cove, waiting to take care of him.'

Barbara said nothing. Kate shifted her weight; her legs

were beginning to ache now, and she still had the walk to the bus stop to negotiate, and then the walk back up Bow Hill. 'Mum, it doesn't have to be like this. I know we've had our differences, I know you disapprove of some of the choices I've made in the past – hell, I disapprove of some of the choices I've made! But I'm older now. I'm a mother. I've been through a lot, and I've spent the last year of my life in hospital. Do you think you could cut me some slack? Couldn't we come to some kind of arrangement, you and I? In Sam's best interests? Couldn't you put your own feelings to one side for long enough to do that?'

'But, Kate,' Barbara said, smiling sweetly, 'that is exactly what I am doing. All of this is for Samuel's benefit, and we are making arrangements. And as I said to your social worker –' she spoke as though social worker was a dirty word '– you may visit Samuel on Wednesday, and then twice a week after that. And once a date is set, we'll let the court decide.'

'Twice a week!' Kate swore under her breath. Elizabeth had kept that part of the arrangement to herself. 'That is outrageous.' She shook her head violently, aware of a pounding in her chest, of the rising of bile in her throat.

Barbara got up slowly, not scraping the chair across the tiles, but lifting it so as to make no noise at all. She crossed to the sink and filled a tall glass with tap water. Kate would have preferred noise, would have preferred shouting and recriminations – all the normal things that families did; the kinds of things that led to reconciliation, to a clearing of the air. The kind of thing her family had never managed to achieve.

'You may come and see Samuel on Wednesday,' Barbara repeated, sipping genteelly from the glass.

'By the way, Mum, his name isn't Samuel. It's Sam. Sam Steiner. It says so on his birth certificate. Or have you had that changed, too?'

'Does it really?' Barbara mused, turning down her mouth at the corners. 'How interesting. Well, no matter. He answers to Samuel now.'

A sound in the hallway caught Kate's attention, and she turned, suddenly fearful that Sam had woken up and heard them arguing. But it wasn't Sam. It was a man Kate hardly recognised. His skin was ashen, his eyes oddly sunken, his once imposing frame now a shadow inside a tweed jacket and navy slacks.

He said, 'Why, hello, Kate!'

Behind them, Barbara dropped her glass on the floor. They turned, all three of them, and stared at the wreckage.

***

Her father sat with his back to her, looking out over his immaculately kept garden. Kate made a bet with herself that her parents had a gardener: a man from the village who was paid a pittance to keep their own little patch of England looking at its very best. The man's wife probably came in and cleaned for them, too.

'Dad,' she said, standing in the doorway, unwilling to commit herself to actually being in the same room as him just yet. He spun around in his chair.

'Kate,' he said, affecting both surprise and pleasure. 'All freshened up now?'

She nodded and sat stiffly on the wicker sofa with orange tapestry cushions. The room, with its three glass walls and glass ceiling, was stiflingly hot. She focused her attention on her hands and steadied her breathing. The last time she'd been in here, Sam had been playing at her feet, with all the plans she had for taking him home with her and starting to build a new life with him still alive in her heart.

The last time she'd been in a room with this man she had said words no daughter should have to speak.

She took a shallow breath, and looked down at her hands.

'Ah, Kate.' Her father got out of his chair and came to sit next to her on the cane sofa. She tried hard not to shrink away from him. 'It is good to see you. You didn't need to run out like that just now, you know. I'm not a monster. I should have been here last week when you came to see little Samuel. Your mother, well, you know how she is. She always ...' He tailed off, his gaze wandering back towards the garden. Kate braced herself, but clearly he had decided against going any further down that road.

'Why, Kate,' he said suddenly, peering at her out of those strangely sunken eyes. 'You've changed so much! You're so thin and pale. What did they do to you at that hospital?' He shook his head as if bewildered. 'Still, you're here now, that's all that matters. Got yourself set up nearby with a place to stay already, your mother tells me. That really is an achievement for ...' he paused, apparently struggling to find the right words. Kate knew he had been about to say, 'For someone like you'.

'For anyone,' he finished. He sank back into the sofa as though exhausted.

So, that was how it was going to be. He was going to try and make it easy for both of them, try and brush everything under the carpet. Kate wondered whether guilt had finally caught up with him, or whether this was just another form of denial.

'Your mother and I were so worried about you when you walked out. How could you just fall off the face of the earth like that? Your mother was very distressed.'

'I didn't fall off the face of the earth. I was in Manchester.'

But she knew that to him it amounted to the same

thing. He mumbled something, and shook his head again. Then he reached to the floor and came up with a jar of mints. He offered the jar to Kate.

'No,' she said. 'No, thank you.'

Kate looked at her father as he bent down to return the jar to the floor. She was taken aback once again by what she saw. He looked so much smaller than she remembered, for one thing. In her mind, whenever she had thought about him during all these years, he was always at least six feet tall, if not taller. And he was solid – not exactly well-built but he had a presence to him, one that made other people respectful, sometimes uncomfortable. She wondered now whether this had been all in her mind. The man sitting by her side, as far away as was possible on such a small sofa, was shorter and skinnier, shrunken in every way. But it occurred to her that her memories of him came entirely from the perspective of a child.

Looking at him now, Kate found it hard to believe he was the same man who had once beaten her mother so badly that her arm had been broken in four places. The same man who had once so frightened his five-year-old daughter she had tried to drag her bookcase across her room to shut him out.

She realised he was speaking, his words failing to make it all the way across the years to reach her ears. With effort she pulled herself back to the present. He was asking her about her plans. Was she intending to stay in Corrin Cove for a while?

Kate shook her head incredulously. 'Of course I'm staying. At least until I get Sam back home with me where he belongs.'

She expected an argument, or worse. But all he said was, 'Right. Good. Well, that's all sorted then.'

What was sorted? Had she missed something here?

'So you're happy for me to see Sam?' she asked.

43

'Of course! He is your son. We can't stop you seeing him, Kate.' He smiled at her, those glassy eyes, those stretched lips. Her father. A stranger. Her reached out and touched her hand. She shivered. 'Don't worry,' he said. 'Everything is going to be fine.'

Chapter 7

The idea had come to Barbara the following morning. It started as a tiny thought, niggling at her, refusing to let go. It was a bad idea. It was a brilliant idea.

It was a very, very bad idea. But it had the potential to solve all her problems. Particularly now it looked as though David had decided to take up with the opposition.

Time for her to get an ally of her own.

Looking around the library, Barbara wished she still lived in a time when it was a librarian's main duty to say 'Shush' as often as possible. She had come into St Austell, not wanting to be seen by anyone who recognised her at the local library in Corrin Cove – and definitely not wanting to risk being seen by Kate, whom she knew was an avid reader. The place was too big for her liking, too noisy for comfort; the rowdy group of kids at the computer next to hers were extremely off-putting and had responded to Barbara's own shushing with hysterical laughter.

Outrageous. She could have used the computer at home, of course, but that was in David's study and she might have found herself in the awkward position of having to tell him what she was doing. She knew next to nothing about computers – there was probably a way for him to tell what she'd been looking at, which would lead to all sorts of awkward questions. That would never do. Better to suffer the public library and try and make the best of it.

Surfing the Internet was not an activity Barbara had indulged in often. She knew that Margaret at the health club liked to order her groceries 'online' but couldn't see the point of this herself. David was always buying this or that from the web – mainly things to do with golf or first editions of boring old books. But she knew it had more important uses than retail therapy. She had heard all about the Internet's magical ability to help anyone search for anything.

What she was searching for was people. Or, more specifically, one person. Evan Williams. Father of Samuel; on-again, off-again boyfriend of her daughter for over a decade. He was out there somewhere, and Barbara intended to find him. The only problem was, she had absolutely no idea where to start.

So far she had found the online version of the phone book and typed his name into the little box. The search for E. Williams in the Manchester area produced more than twenty names, but short of phoning each one personally, Barbara had no idea how to narrow it down. Kate had told her that Evan dropped out of 'the scene', as she so charmingly put it, just before Barbara came to stay when Samuel was only a few weeks old; she had been sure he'd moved away so as to avoid all contact with Kate and his baby. This wouldn't have surprised Barbara at all. Although she'd never met him, she didn't have a high regard for someone who could abandon his own child, no matter how annoying Kate might have been. But she thought she knew enough about human nature to think it fairly certain that he would gravitate back towards his old hunting ground eventually. It took guts and stamina to start up from scratch in a new location; she doubted Evan had it in him.

The library's home page on the computer had its own search facility, so Barbara thought she'd try this next.

She typed in the name carefully. 2,120,000 results. That was not narrowing it down. She huffed and sat back in her chair. Bloody computers. She should have known not to trust them.

'Are you okay?' a voice to her left asked quietly. Barbara swung round. She hadn't noticed that the rabble had gone and been replaced by an earnest-looking young man in black-framed glasses.

'Yes, thank you,' she said automatically.

The man nodded and turned back to his own console. Barbara looked again at her screen. She tried retyping Evan's name, this time with the surname first. It made no difference at all. She tutted loudly, annoyed with herself as much as the computer.

A second or two later the young man spoke again. 'Are you sure I can't help you with anything?'

Barbara told him politely no. And then she thought, why not? She was certain Kate had people fawning around her all the time.

She gave the young man her best, most helpless smile. 'Actually, maybe you can. You don't know anything about computers, do you? It's my son. He's missing, you see, and I'm just desperate to find him …'

Chapter 8

The box arrived on Saturday morning, delivered by courier to the house on Bow Hill. Marie stood at the bottom of the stairs and called for Kate, her voice high-pitched with excitement.

'Something for you,' she cried. 'Something very big!'

The box was indeed enormous, the size of a washing machine or freezer. Kate had been sitting up in bed, gazing out of the dusty window, watching the progress of a black cat over the random collection of fences that separated the terraced gardens of Bow Hill. At the sound of Marie's voice she climbed out of bed, pulled on her thin dressing gown, and reached for her crutch.

She stepped gingerly down the stairs, holding onto the banister with her free hand. The courier was still in the narrow hallway, forced to stand far too close to a delighted Marie, who was leaning on the box to scrawl her name onto an electronic pad. You could tell she was taking her time over it, enjoying every minute.

'I wonder what it is?' Marie said. Kate shook her head and edged closer. The courier grabbed the device as soon as Marie let go of the stylus and headed for the door. Marie laughed and waved to him, then she turned to Kate and clapped her hands.

'He can bring me a box any day of the week,' she said, grinning.

'Marie, you are incorrigible. He's at least half your age.'

'Who cares about age when he's got muscles like that?'

'What about Big Tony? Doesn't he have muscles too?'

Marie smiled wistfully. 'He certainly does, my dear. In all the right places.'

The box took up most of the hallway. Kate scanned the label; the return address was in Manchester. It must be her things out of storage. So this was what her whole life amounted to, this was all that was left. When you thought about it that way, it didn't seem such a big box after all.

Just then a key turned in the door. Kate looked up in surprise, and then found herself unaccountably reddening when she saw Patrick squeezing into the narrow hallway.

'You dirty stop out,' Marie said, her eyes glinting. 'Putting in an all-nighter on the sly. I didn't know he had it in him,' she added, turning to wink at Kate. 'And such a quiet, mild-mannered boy.'

Patrick pressed himself back against the door, his expression dubious.

'Oh, come on past,' Marie said, pulling in her stomach. 'You can just about get through.'

Kate breathed in his scent of the outdoors as he passed her, his chest level with her face, his arm briefly brushing hers. The contact was electric, a shock wave through her body, filling her with heat. For a moment she felt a little lightheaded, and she leaned on the box for support.

'Who was the lucky lady?' Marie cried as Patrick began to mount the stairs. He turned and grinned. Kate noticed again how his face seemed to come alive when he smiled. She seemed hyper-aware of every detail of his face, his hair, the shape of his body.

'You know perfectly well I've been at work,' he told Marie, shaking his head in mock despair. 'Honestly, you'll give our new resident the worst kind of impression.'

His accent was mildly Scottish, only a hint, but it gave his voice a soft, melodic note.

'And I imagine you are very concerned about making the right impression on our lovely Kate, aren't you?' Marie teased. Kate felt her cheeks growing pink again; she could see that Patrick was embarrassed too. He started up the stairs again, but Marie hadn't finished with him yet.

'Hold your horses! We need a big strong man to carry this up to Kate's room. You can't expect us feeble ladies to do it.'

Marie gave the box an almighty shove, but it didn't budge. She winked again at Kate as Patrick lifted the box with ease. Marie followed him up the stairs, making swooning gestures behind his back while Kate threw her friend warning glares and tried very hard not to fixate her eyes on Patrick's very attractive behind. The poor man. How he'd lived in this house with Marie as his landlady for over two years was beyond Kate's comprehension.

Once the box was safely installed in Kate's room, Marie bustled off to find scissors to cut the tape and Patrick made himself scarce. Suddenly, Kate found she couldn't wait for the scissors. She had no idea what she would find in there – she had spent so much time thinking about Sam, focusing on Sam, she'd hardly given a thought to her life before. She grabbed her keys and stabbed them into the brown tape, dragging them along the join until the top of the box flew open. She lifted the flaps and peered inside.

Whoever had put this lot into storage had packed it with care. Polystyrene chips filled the space, flying up around her as she grabbed the first thing her fingers touched, landing on the carpet like snow around her feet.

The inside smelt of a musty garage, but didn't feel damp. She pulled out a plastic vacuum-packed bag that looked to be full of clothes and laid it on the floor. Next came a painted wooden jewellery box, bringing with it a sharp stab of memory – Evan, reflected behind her in their bedroom mirror, doing up the silver choker he had bought for her birthday. She opened the jewellery box and rifled through it. The silver choker wasn't there; nor were any of her better pieces of jewellery. Well, of course they weren't. Everything of value must have been taken during the break-in.

'Oh, sweetie, I see you've managed without me.' Marie arrived back in Kate's room, out of breath and holding a pair of kitchen scissors. Kate looked up. She had sunk to the floor, clutching the jewellery box to her chest, pulled back through time by her memories of another life. She started blankly at Marie: who was this woman, and what was she doing here? A stab of fear shot through her at the sight of the scissors, but then her memory reoriented itself and the fear ebbed away. Kate shook her head. Corrin Cove. Bow Hill. Sam.

Sam.

She said, 'Marie, please don't be offended but I'd really rather do this alone. These are my things, you see. From ... from before.'

Marie nodded, and then she did something that Kate thought was extraordinary. She bent down and kissed Kate lightly on top of her head. 'My dear thing,' she said, 'you know where I am if you need me.'

Once Marie had gone, and Kate had heard her footsteps on the stairs, the door to her own rooms on the ground floor slamming cheerfully behind her, she reached into the box again. She laid out each item, one by one, on the worn carpet. A plastic file full of out-of-date paperwork and unpaid bills; a photograph album with curling cellophane pockets and a ramshackle handful of prints shoved inside; three pairs of shoes, snuggled together heel to toe, and a stack of clothes wrapped in tissue. Another flat-packed bag of linen; a stack of paperback novels; a collection of postcards, bound together with elastic bands. A plastic carrier bag of toiletries; a grubby-looking bright green handbag and various belts and scarves. Near the bottom were two cardboard cartons filled with ornaments wrapped in newspaper.

Kate unwrapped one sheet of newspaper and looked at the date. She scanned the headlines, feeling like a time-traveller, feeling lightheaded and a little strange. She recognised everything, and yet none of it seemed to be her, somehow. It seemed to belong to a different Kate, an earlier version. A Kate who collected china owls, who read books for fun, who bought shampoo for colour-treated hair. She ran a hand through her hair and wondered whether someone had cut it for her while she was asleep. Any colour had grown out or washed out a long time ago.

She reached into the carton again and pulled out a wooden concertina sewing box. The tiny hinges squeaked as she opened both sides of the lid. Inside, a mass of thread and bobbins and ribbons and pins greeted her in cheerful chaos. She ran her hand through the rainbow colours and smiled sadly. Here was the Kate she remembered. Sewing had filled the void in her life when she and Evan began to drift apart. She'd discovered a natural talent for following patterns, loving the feel of crinkly brown paper pinned to fabric, delighting in the way each pattern piece fitted together like a jigsaw puzzle.

She thrust her arms into the cavernous box, rummaging through the remainder of the polystyrene chippings. It must be in here. In fact, that would have been what made the box so heavy. Her fingers touched something solid and cold, and she breathed out in relief. It was here. She felt her way around it, lovingly stroking the machine's curved bulk. It was too cumbersome for her to pull out of the box herself. She looked around, biting her lip, then had an idea. Leverage was what she needed. Suddenly imbued with an energy she hadn't felt for the longest time, Kate dragged the massive box over to the bed. She stood and wedged her body against it, then she reached down again, gripping the sewing machine with both hands, and heaved. It moved about an inch.

'Damn it.' She just wasn't strong enough. In her old life she could have done this. She remembered heaving the ancient machine up the stairs to her flat and installing it on the kitchen table. How she had loved to sit there sewing while Sam gurgled in his playpen or sat in the high chair by her side. She had made him more outfits than he could ever wear, had spent hours online searching for new patterns, becoming a regular fixture at the haberdasher's she found in one of the older, less affluent parts of Manchester's sprawling centre.

But now, even with her arms strengthened from all these weeks hauling herself around, she was too weak to get her most prized possession out of a cardboard box.

'No,' she said out loud, not caring if Marie or Patrick heard her talking to herself. She tried to picture Joseph's challenging face, his tone of blithe instruction. He would tell her it was all in her mind. He would say she could do it if she really wanted to.

Kate set to work. She stuffed the polystyrene chippings back into the box, batting at them as they flew up around her face and got stuck in her hair. Once the sewing machine was well and truly packed in, she carefully lowered the box onto its side. From this position she could simply slide the machine out, and then righten it once it was clear of the box. She looked down at her handiwork, brushing the white chippings off her legs and her arms, then she tipped the nearly empty box upside down, laughing again at the cascade of snow, feeling free and strong. Her hands itched to get hold of some fabric, to begin that satisfying process of cutting and matching, tacking and hemming. She picked up a loose bobbin and rolled it around in her palm.

What if she were to start making clothes again? Or what if she offered some kind of alteration service locally? It might be a way to earn some money, a way give her and Sam a better start in their new life together. A way to get back on her feet.

Kate jumped up, her scalp tingling with excitement. Marie would know people – didn't she go to that slimming group at the community centre? There might be successful dieters in need of clothes taking in, and she could put up a poster in the newsagent's and advertise for customers, start off small and grow by word-of-mouth. She could check out the competition, find out what they charged, make sure she wasn't too expensive, but just add that personal touch ...

She ran her hand through her collection of threads and allowed the nugget of excitement to grow. Her room sat in disarray, packaging and clothes and boxes strewn by her feet, but Kate didn't care. A plan was forming, and for the first time in years she felt strong. Better than strong. She felt in control of her future.

Chapter 9

The weekend passed in a flurry of activity, and while it didn't drive thoughts of Sam from her mind, Kate found that having something to do helped her cope with missing him just a little bit better. She enlisted Marie's help in setting up the sewing machine, and Marie had shot straight upstairs to get Patrick, who appeared on Sunday morning carrying a fold-out table he'd found at the junk shop on the Parade. Marie had her own contribution: a boxful of old curtains and a stack of vintage bedding.

'They were my mother's,' Marie explained, throwing the fabric onto Kate's bed with no care at all. 'I've never had a clue what to do with them.'

Kate picked up a set of curtains – sunshine yellow with a pattern of green and gold leaves – and stroked them in awe. 'These are silk,' she said. 'They must be worth a fortune.' The fabric was soft against her cheek; they smelt of perfume, the flowery kind that no one wore anymore.

Marie shrugged. 'Well, I don't want them. Maybe you could make me a dress or something,' she added, laughing as though the very idea was completely impossible. But Kate nodded slowly.

A swift assessment of the contents of her storage box had produced very few wearable clothes for Kate herself. Most of the items she had thought to be clothing when they were vacuum-packed in the transparent storage bags had turned out to be either her own collection of fabric scraps or the bits and pieces she'd made for Sam during the first few months of his life. These were currently hanging in Sam's room, or in what would soon be his room, even though it was doubtful they'd actually fit him. Kate's favourite piece was a sailor's outfit she'd constructed for Sam when he was six months old. She remembered that she had used offcuts from an old shirt Evan left behind, and some navy cord from a skirt she sourced in a charity shop. The buttons had been scavenged from a jacket left behind from Kate's clubbing days, the ship design perfect for the tiny outfit. Kate had sat at the kitchen table for hours, working in the light of an angle-poise lamp clamped to the edge of the chipped Formica, sewing on the buttons so securely they could never be pulled off by tiny hands. The sailor suit was her finest piece, and she longed to show it to Sam. She wondered whether he would remember it – maybe not consciously, but perhaps the memory of the sense of it, of how she had made it just for him, would have lived on inside him somehow.

There was no sign of the angle-poise lamp, but the table Patrick had bought for her was practically the twin of her old one. Kate tried to pay him for it, but Patrick wouldn't hear of it.

'It cost buttons,' he told her. He was under the table, replacing a blown fuse in the socket she needed for the sewing machine. Kate watched him from her perch on the bed. He was lovely, there was no denying it. Even in his Sunday scruffs – loose T-shirt and greying shorts – he had a presence that made Kate aware of his every movement. He was different from Evan, different from any man Kate had met before.

Patrick was nice.

'Well, that's lucky, because I have buttons,' she said lightly. 'I can pay you with them.'

He eased out from under the table and looked up at her, his eyes twinkling. 'Okay. It's a deal. You can pay me in buttons.'

Was he flirting with her? Kate had no idea. But if she couldn't read his signals, she was even less adept at reading her own.

***

On Monday morning, Kate dressed in her smartest pair of jeans and a white blouse she remembered buying from a Manchester boutique during one of her flush spells.

'Morning,' Marie said, magically appearing in her doorway just as Kate reached the bottom of the stairs. 'Off out, are we?'

'Physio,' Kate explained with a grimace.

'Ah, yes. Hold on a minute.' Marie disappeared back into her part of the house, which Kate had yet to explore, but which she imagined to be decorated in bright, gaudy colours with lamps shrouded in tasselled scarves and cushions plumping up every conceivable surface. She tapped her fingers against the worn wooden banister, then glanced at her watch. Her appointment was in fifty minutes. She'd be pressed to make it to the bus stop in time if she hung around much longer.

'Right, we're all set,' Marie said, emerging in a cloud of perfume, an umbrella shoved under her arm.

'For what?' Kate asked, eyeing the umbrella. It was at least twenty-five degrees outside, and humid as hell.

'For our trip to the big smoke, of course.' Marie linked arms with Kate and pulled her down the hall. 'I thought I'd tag along, you don't mind do you? I need to get my hair cut. It's just totally out of control.'

Kate smiled, taking in Marie's lacquered hair, styled today into something resembling a beehive. She pitied the hairdresser tasked with putting a comb to that.

On Bow Hill, the sun had turned everything hazy and the very pavement felt as though it was melting under their feet.

'Marie,' Kate said seriously, 'I really don't think you'll need an umbrella. Unless there's some freak weather system moving in that none of the rest of us can see.'

She tilted her head to look out across the horizon. The haze was even stronger there, and the sky stretched on over blues and greens, broken only by the random pattern of a fishing boat or one of the leisure cruisers that sometimes moored off Corrin Cove. Her shirt was already stuck to her back and they'd only been outdoors for a minute.

Marie giggled, then opened the umbrella – an enormous affair, with frilled edges and peacock blue circles and a bright pink handle. 'Silly girl,' she said, tipping the umbrella over her shoulder and nearly knocking Kate off the pavement in the process. 'This is a parasol, not a brolly. I have to look after my complexion, you know. UV rays are hell for wrinkles.' She peered at Kate's pale face, then shook her head. 'You don't need to worry about that for a few years yet. But mark my words – no man wants a woman with skin like leather.'

They set off down the hill arm in arm, and Kate found that she could simply carry her crutch in her free hand, so solid was Marie's support. And after a while she found that she wasn't leaning on her friend much at all. The sun lit up the world as brightly as a hundred watt bulb, and Marie lit up her mind with her chatter and her gossip and her seemingly endless supply of warmth. Eschewing the bus – 'Public transport is just so sticky, don't you find?' – Marie insisted on paying for a taxi into St Austell, citing Kate's crutch as reason enough to make it worthwhile. Kate found herself deposited outside the medical centre fifteen minutes later, with a promise that Marie would swing by and pick her up in two hours' time.

'Bye,' Kate called, waving to Marie's cheerful face pressed up against the taxi's rear window. She turned and regarded the medical centre warily, then glanced again at her watch. She was early, but that was okay. Without Marie's buoyant presence, Kate could feel her mood slipping dangerously. On the wall just inside the entrance was a sign for the cafeteria. She would buy coffee and cake, she decided, and try not to think about anything at all. One step at a time, Joseph had said. One foot in front of the other. Look at me now, she thought, pushing open the door to the cafeteria, hardly leaning on her crutch at all. Maybe Joseph was right – maybe it was all in the mind. She wondered if that theory applied to every part of life. If she could apply the same force of will to getting Sam back as she had to learning to walk again, she might just be in with a chance.

***

Nico lacked Joseph's steely-eyed determination, but within an hour Kate had been put through her paces and was declared to be doing 'Very well indeed, considering.' Kate thought this was fair praise, and asked about moving to a stick.

'Maybe,' Nico said, but this clearly meant yes because he produced a selection from a cupboard in the therapy room and proceeded to have Kate walk up and down with each of them in turn until she'd found one that felt right. She chose a metal-tipped walking cane that was made, according to Nico, from blackthorn wood. She loved the feel of its curved handle in her palm; loved how it flexed a little as she leaned on it.

'This is the one,' she said, smiling, and Nico nodded,

his expression serious. He gestured for her to sit, and began to scribble notes onto a fresh page in her file.

'It goes on computer later,' he explained, nodding towards an ancient-looking computer screen collecting dust in the corner. 'We're not behind the times,' he added with just a touch of defensiveness. Kate couldn't care less. She stroked her cane and wondered whether she'd be allowed to keep it once she was fully recovered.

'So, Kate Steiner,' Nico said with a smile, 'tell me how you are settling in down here.'

She gave a tiny shrug, unsure how to answer. 'The house social services found for me is really nice. I mean, the lady who owns it is nice.'

'And your son?' Nico asked, his gaze unwavering. 'Have you seen him? It's all in your file,' he added when Kate blanched. 'I don't mean to pry. Your therapist in Manchester, he wrote it all down.'

'Sure.' Kate swallowed over a lump in her throat. 'I've seen my son. And he'll be coming to live with me very soon.'

'Good.' Nico smiled. 'Are there any other symptoms you've noticed since being discharged? Physical or otherwise – you must let your GP know if you notice anything untoward.'

There was something, but Kate was loath to bring it up. Besides, Nico was her physical therapist, not her doctor, as he himself had just pointed out. She hesitated, but then decided to mention it anyway. He'd probably tell her it was nothing, and then she could just forget about it.

'I get nightmares,' she confessed. 'I mean, really bad ones. I don't like to sleep much anyway – I lost so much time to sleep, it doesn't feel right to just lie down and close my eyes. I suppose that sounds stupid to you.'

Nico said nothing. Kate sighed, then carried on.

'So, when I do let myself fall asleep I just have these

awful nightmares. I think they ... I think they're about the attack. At least, that's all I can come up with to explain them.'

Nico glanced at her file again. 'You were hit on the head by an intruder.' He made it sound oddly mundane. Kate nodded, not trusting herself to speak for fear she might start crying. It was being in a hospital environment again, she told herself. It brought up all the feelings of insecurity and helplessness she thought she'd left behind in Manchester.

'Do you see your attacker in your nightmares?' Nico asked, leaning forward and propping his elbows on his knees. Like all physiotherapists Kate had ever met, he wore tracksuit bottoms and a T-shirt, making him look younger than perhaps he was, like a grown-up boy playing sports at school.

She shook her head. 'No face. Just this sense of someone behind me. It's daytime, and I'm in my kitchen. It's not the exact same kitchen, you understand, but it is where I live. Where I lived, I mean. And there's someone in the room with me. I can't hear him, but I can sense him. Just standing there. And I'm too afraid to turn around. In my dream, my legs are weak and my body is useless, just how it was when I first woke up from the coma. And Sam is there. Sam is sitting in his playpen, chattering away, gurgling and laughing and chewing on his plastic train, and all the time I'm just staring at him, unable to move a muscle. So scared. Just so afraid that something is going to happen to him, and if I just stay very still he might be okay.' The tears came now, just as Kate had known they would, but there was nothing she could do about it. She wiped her face on her sleeve, just one quick swipe, hoping Nico wouldn't notice. 'In my dream,' she said, 'I can sense the man is behind me, he's standing right there.' She pointed behind her now, and then turned her head involuntarily, as though there might actually be somebody there. Stupid. She chastised herself, and looked at Nico to see whether he wanted her to carry on.

'And?' he said. 'What happens next?'

'Nothing. I mean, it's just this terrible, paralysing fear. I wake up sweating, and then I curse myself for going to sleep in the first place. If I don't sleep I don't have the nightmare. So it's easy enough to avoid.' She laughed, but Nico's face remained serious.

'You need to sleep,' he said. 'There is no option of not sleeping, no matter how long you were comatose, no matter how much time you feel you lost. You will sleep, and it will help you get better. This nightmare, it may be psychosomatic – a reaction to the feelings of helplessness and fear you had during and after the incident. Or ...'

He tailed off, regarding Kate with an odd expression. She opened her mouth to prompt him to continue, then closed it again. She wasn't sure she wanted to hear what he was going to say.

'Or, Kate, it might be that you are merely remembering. And that you are afraid to turn around in your dream because if you do, you will see who it is who did this terrible thing to you.'

It wasn't as though the thought hadn't occurred to her already, but now, hearing Nico say the words out loud, Kate felt a prickly sensation on her neck. She shook her head, and forced a smile onto her face.

'I'm sure it's just stress,' she said. 'Nothing more.'

She left Nico's treatment room with an appointment for the following week, and waited outside the medical centre for Marie.

Was it possible that she had seen her attacker? If so, why didn't she remember who it was? If she could recall a face, or any detail whatsoever, it would help the police to identify who had done this, and if they could find that person they might be able to recover the rest of her things. More importantly, if the police could arrest her attacker, Kate might be able to prove that the cannabis hidden in her flat was not hers at all, but had been put there by someone else. But why? To make her look bad? But who would want to do that? Perhaps they'd been disturbed and had hidden the drugs with the intention of coming back later. But disturbed by who? Not by Kate – the police report had been clear that Kate had been at the kitchen table when the attacker struck. If only she could remember what had happened ...

If only the nightmares weren't so terrifying that she woke up the very minute she began to turn around.

Chapter 10

In the taxi on the way home, Marie asked Kate why she didn't get in touch with Sam's father now that she was out of hospital and fighting to get custody of her own son again.

'It's not exactly custody,' Kate explained. Although it might as well be, she thought, for all the rights she seemed to have.

'Look,' Marie said, straightening up the myriad shopping bags that fell over again every time the taxi rounded a corner, 'I realise you can't just waltz in there and drag him out of your parents' house. I know you have to tread softly, for his sake. But surely if his dad were here too, they wouldn't have a leg to stand on. They couldn't argue that you couldn't cope, or whatever it is they're saying, if there were two of you looking out for little Sam.'

Kate sighed. 'Marie, you don't know the half of it. Things would be ten times worse for me and Sam if Evan were here, believe me. He's bad news. No, really,' she added, seeing Marie's sceptical expression. 'He is. You wouldn't want him living in your house, put it that way.'

'He'd be quite welcome if you vouched for him,' Marie insisted.

'Well, that won't happen,' Kate said, shivering involuntarily. 'Look, I was young when I met him. Young and stupid. He swept me off my feet –'

'So he's a bit of a charmer, is he?'

'Yes, but not in a good way.' She could see that Marie didn't get it. 'Okay, listen to this. Evan had a friend, a guy called Jake. They decided to set up a business together – Evan was always off on some harebrained scheme or other, I don't think he ever had a real, honest job in his life. So, Jake puts up the money and Evan takes off abroad to buy a load of stock. He'd sourced a place in Estonia, he said, that produced computer parts dirt cheap. Meanwhile, Jake was down at the local ProntoPrint getting sorted with business cards and flyers, and he found a unit on an industrial estate where they could store their stock. They'd even taken on an apprentice from the technical college, all totally above board.' Kate looked out of the taxi window at the sweeping coastline and allowed her mind to slip backwards. She'd been so hopeful that time, convinced that Evan would come good.

She should have known better.

'So,' Marie prompted. 'What happened?'

'You think you know where this is going,' Kate continued with a sigh. 'Someone like Evan, you think he'd just disappear with the money, go on a bender, gamble the lot, something like that.'

'He didn't?'

Kate shook her head. 'Sadly not. What he did was much worse. The electronics were a cover for another deal that Evan was working on. He used them to get "merchandise" into the country – you can imagine what kind of merchandise. Worse still, he used Jake's name to do the deal, used his passport to travel under, left a trail a mile wide for the authorities. He screwed the Estonian dealers out of their cut, then hot-footed it back to England with the money and the shipment. By the time the police got involved, Evan was nowhere to be found.'

'Oh, dear.'

'Jake, however, was here large as life, with a storage

unit full of dodgy electronics absolutely reeking of traces of Class A drugs.'

'Kate! How on earth did you get mixed up with a character like that?'

'I told you,' Kate said glumly. 'I was young and impressionable. When I met him I had no idea what he was capable of. And he did have a good side. He was fun, he could be caring – like really, really attentive. And he was very sexy. When Evan looked at you the world seemed to stop turning. It was kind of –'

'Irresistible,' Marie finished. 'Yes, I know. Big Tony is just the same.'

'Hardly.' Kate laughed. 'Believe me, in the lovable rogue stakes, your Tony wins hands down. There's not much to love about Evan.'

Marie fell quiet by her side, and Kate sank into her thoughts again. It was true that he had been irresistible. And very, very charming. And Kate had been so deeply in love that nothing Evan did affected her for the longest time. Until she finally grew up.

'What did you do, Kate, before you had Sam?' Marie had her purchases gathered up around her legs again; they weren't far from the promenade.

'I worked in a bar for a while. Did some cleaning. Just anything, really. I've never been afraid of hard work,' she added, wondering why Marie thought it necessary to ask. Probably worried about the rent. 'Listen,' Kate said earnestly, 'I'm serious about this alteration service, about standing on my own two feet. And if it doesn't work out I'll get a job. I'll do anything, work around Sam as soon as he starts nursery. I know the benefits cover my rent for now, but I'm not a freeloader. I never have been.'

Marie shook her head, but before she could speak the taxi lurched to a halt and all the shopping bags tipped over. Kate dived forward to help repack them, glad to be out of her landlady's inquisitive gaze. The truth – that she was qualified for nothing and fit for even less – smarted a lot more back here in Corrin Cove than it ever had in the streets of Manchester.

***

By Wednesday Kate was so desperate to see Sam it was like a physical ache. The morning brought a heavy fog that hung over a flat grey sea, tightening Kate's chest when she went out for her walk. All the way along the promenade her stomach rolled and churned. She had a bad feeling, but couldn't pinpoint why. Things were progressing okay; in fact, the process of getting Sam back had moved up a notch. Elizabeth had phoned that very morning to confirm that the application to discharge the guardianship order had been lodged with the court.

'Are you certain there is no chance of doing this amicably?' Elizabeth had asked again. 'The court prefers a mediated solution in these cases.'

Mediate it then, Kate had wanted to say. She knew it wasn't Elizabeth's fault, but why was everyone talking to her as though she could do anything about it? Hadn't she tried to talk to her mother, to find some common ground?

'If by amicable you mean that I simply agree to give up my son and visit him a couple of times a week then no, I don't think that's very likely,' she said instead. She heard Elizabeth's weary sigh. 'Look,' Kate continued, flicking her hair back over her shoulders and setting her jaw determinedly, 'I'm happy for them to see Sam as often as they like when he comes home to live with me. They've done a great job, and it's not as though I'm ungrateful. I'm not saying they're monsters,' she added. 'It's them who have a problem with me, not the other way around.'

Kate shifted the phone to her other ear, wondering whether she was being entirely honest with Elizabeth. The knot in her stomach hadn't eased after seeing her father on Monday; if anything it had only grown larger. Could he really have changed? And if so, what did that mean for her and Sam?

'Well, that's all good,' Elizabeth said, winding up the call. 'It will look good to the court that you are being reasonable, that you're the more moderate party. Take care now. Enjoy your freedom – you'll have Sam back very soon, I'm sure.'

Those words had been like a balm for her soul. Kate had drunk them in, then replayed them over and over. When Marie came out, magically appearing as soon as the call was over, Kate had shared them, spoken the words out loud, and together they had started to make plans for Sam's room, deciding what colour it should be painted, what kind of furniture he'd need.

'I have a cot in the attic!' Marie exclaimed. 'I'll get Patrick to fetch it down as soon as he gets in from work.'

For once, Kate hadn't argued.

Her mother was courteous but cold when Kate arrived at the house.

'Sam is in his bedroom,' Barbara said. 'You shouldn't have any trouble finding it. It's your old room.'

Upstairs, Kate paused in the doorway, overwhelmed all over again at the sight of her son, at the solid reality of him. She approached him and lowered herself onto the carpet by his side. As usual, he accepted her presence with no surprise, merely passing her a slightly sticky green crayon before continuing to scratch out his own piece of art.

As they played, Kate relaxed and began to enjoy herself. He was a clever child, and clearly sociable, unlike she had been at his age. Chatting easily, Sam pointed out his favourite toys and told her how he was going to be a builder when he grew up. Kate felt herself brimming over with liquid love, like someone had opened her up and poured it in and didn't know when to stop.

He called her father Pops and her mother Nana, much to Kate's surprise – she had expected them to be more formal, more old-fashioned. 'So,' she said, reaching across the tiles to pick up a toy rabbit with chewed-looking ears, 'do Pops or Nana ever shout at you?'

The boy looked unsure and Kate corrected herself hurriedly. 'I mean, do they tell you off sometimes?' She smiled warmly to put him at ease, holding the rabbit out for him to take.

'Only when Sam bad,' he said quietly, taking the toy from her and cuddling it briefly to his face.

'I bet you're not bad very often though, are you?'

'No.' His voice was smaller and more timid than before, and Kate hoped with all her heart that she hadn't upset him with her questions. But then he looked up at her, eyes bright again. 'Shout at each other,' he announced triumphantly. 'Very lots.'

'Do they?' Kate turned her face away, her heart pounding. That was how it had always started. A row, raised voices, thunder rumbling below the stairs. She had learned to stay in her room, in this room, and be as quiet as a mouse. She was always terrified she might get in the way of one of her father's rages ...

Kate instinctively reached out for Sam, embracing him awkwardly. He allowed her a few seconds then squirmed away, returning to his crayons.

Perhaps the phone call with Elizabeth had unsettled her more than she'd realised. She had said her parents weren't monsters, but for a long time wasn't that exactly what she had thought about them? Kate could see no outward signs that her son was unhappy, but no one had ever noticed any signs in her as a child either. She knew only too well how easy it was to become accustomed to anger and volatility. More than anything, she didn't want this for Sam.

'Don't worry, little man,' she said softly. 'I'll have you out of here in no time.'

Settling back against the foot of the cane sofa, Kate reflected on how easy and comfortable it felt to be here with her son. Did he feel the same? she wondered. What did he think of her visiting like this?

'Sam,' she said, interrupting his flow of constant chatter.

'Henry at play group call me Sam,' he told her. 'Nana call me Samuel.'

'Well, your name is Sam.'

'How you know?'

'Because I'm your mummy,' she said firmly. 'Do you remember I told you that last week? Do you understand what that means?'

'Henry has a mummy.' Sam thrust his fist into his mouth, his eyes wide and surprised.

'And so do you, sweetheart. You can call me mummy if you like.'

'Nana say you call Kate.'

I bet that's not all she's called me, Kate thought glumly. Although by the looks of it, not in front of Sam, which was something to be grateful for.

'Sam, there's something else you need to know. Soon you're going to be coming home with –'

'Kate!' Barbara's voice from the doorway made both of them jump. They turned around, looking up with identical shocked expressions.

Then Sam smiled easily and said, 'Hi, Nana,' while Kate tried to calm her breathing.

'Time to get washed and ready for tea,' Barbara said to Sam, who jumped up eagerly, scattering his crayons all over the floor. He poked his head around his grandmother's legs to look back at Kate.

'She staying for tea?' he asked, pointing. Kate felt such a surge of love for him. Her son. Her own, sweet little boy.

Before she could answer that she would love to have tea with him, her mother butted in. 'No, she isn't. Now, go on, off you go.'

'By-eee,' he sang as he disappeared in the direction of the bathroom. Kate and her mother regarded each other warily. Feeling at a distinct disadvantage sitting on the floor, Kate dropped eye contact and pulled herself upright. She grabbed her new cane and leaned on it.

Kate's father appeared behind Barbara, his dark eyes tired but warm. Barbara spoke to him without taking her gaze off Kate.

'She has been asking the boy all sorts of inappropriate questions. And she was about to tell him that she is taking him home with her. I warned you this would happen. Now we'll have to deal with the fall out.'

'What fall out?' Kate enquired mildly, knowing her blasé tone would only infuriate her mother more.

David looked at the side of his wife's head, then back at Kate. 'What's this?'

'Were you listening behind the door the whole time?' Kate said.

'Just as well I was.' Barbara confronted her husband. 'Well, I hope you're happy now. You said to just leave them alone together, to let them get on with it, and now look what's happened.'

'What kind of inappropriate questions?' he asked, still looking at Kate.

'About whether we argue. About whether we shout at Samuel.' Barbara's face was as tight as a vice. Kate wondered if her mother still suffered from the headaches that had been almost constant when she was a child. She decided that if she did, she probably deserved them.

71

She waited for her father's expression to change from one of confusion to one of anger. She remembered watching him like this as a child, marking his moods the way you'd notice changes in the weather. A storm coming. The gathering clouds. Kate glanced behind her parents, worried that Sam would come back in.

The explosion should have happened by now. Kate could remember so clearly watching their arguments, seeing her mother veering back in the face of his outbursts as if pushed by a sudden wind.

'I'm not scared of you anymore,' she told her father quietly, fingering the brick she had secretly pocketed. 'You can't intimidate me. I'm not a child.'

His mouth opened and closed, his face reddening, the colour creeping up from his collar but leaving patches of white around his mouth. She knew this process well, knew she probably had about three minutes before he began to lose control. Kate turned to her mother.

'I'm leaving now. I don't want to cause a scene – it will only be Sam who suffers, I'm sure. But I'm telling you now, if I ever hear that he –' she indicated her father with a nod of her head '– has so much as raised his voice near my son, I will take Sam out of this house myself, with or without your or the court's say so. Do you understand?'

'You can't take him,' her mother stated flatly. 'I will never, ever let you do that.'

Kate shook her head, incredulous. 'Mum, you're deluded. Once the date comes through you are going to have to come to terms with me, or you'll risk never seeing Sam again.'

Barbara shook her head. The faint smile playing around her lips made Kate feel slightly sick.

'We'll see,' Barbara said. Then she turned and walked slowly down the stairs.

***

Kate found her father in the lounge. Every nerve in her body was screaming at her to leave it alone, just get out of the house, quit while she was ahead. But there it was, that wilful streak again.

He was sitting on the sofa facing the wall, legs crossed, a glass in his hand. A familiar tableau. The smell hit her as she approached, both fresh and stale, assaulting her with a torment of memories.

'He shouldn't be living here with you,' Kate said quietly. Her father said nothing. She couldn't see his face. 'Not if you're still drinking.'

'Ah, Kate,' he said, and then nothing else. For a moment, Kate allowed a spike of worry to enter her heart. He was ill. That was clear to her now. But the spike couldn't penetrate the years of fear and hatred. She turned away and went to find her mother in the kitchen.

'He's very sick, isn't he?' she said quietly. Sam was already eating, sitting in a high chair in front of a wall-mounted TV showing cartoons. She waved to him, but he didn't even glance in her direction.

'I've no idea,' Barbara replied. Kate caught her mother's expression. Weary. Her mother wasn't afraid of him anymore either. Her mother was merely tired of him.

'So, I'll be back to see Sam again on Friday. With or without your permission.'

'Whatever,' Barbara said tiredly.

In the doorway, Kate stopped and looked back. 'Is it the drinking?'

Barbara shook her head, then she looked down at her hands and shrugged.

'You should stop him, Mum. It's not too late for him to change. Look at that cabinet in there – it's full of booze. Throw it away. You shouldn't have so much alcohol around with a child in the house.'

'Oh, you're a fine one to talk,' Barbara retorted.

'Mum,' she said, 'it was the odd bit of pot. And it was Evan who was into it, I only ever dabbled occasionally. Besides, marijuana isn't the same as other drugs.' Even as Kate spoke she could see her mother closing up. There was no distinction in her eyes between smoking pot and lying in a gutter with a needle sticking out of your arm.

'The widest used drug in this country is alcohol, did you know that?' Kate pointed again to her parents' well-stocked drinks cabinet. 'It's far more physically addictive, and more likely to make you violent.' A picture of her father leaning over her, breath like methylated spirits, eyes bloodshot, appeared in Kate's mind and threatened to wreck her composure. She turned back to her mother, her eyes flashing. 'Alcohol just happens to be legal.'

Barbara returned her glare with a challenging one of her own. 'That's hardly the point, is it?'

'Well, Mum, what is? You tell me. I'm sorry you feel I've let you down. I did my best, but the attack, and the drugs that were found in my flat – none of that was my fault. I don't know why you're punishing me. All I want is to take Sam home and get on with my life.'

Her mother, back-lit by the fading sun, gave the tiniest of shrugs. It was the merest suggestion of a movement, but Kate could not mistake her meaning. She crossed the kitchen and kissed Sam on the top of his head.

'Be safe,' she whispered, then she left the house without another word.

Chapter 11

Barbara set the table the same way she had every evening for more years than she cared to remember. Placemats, knives and forks. Dessert spoons, wine glasses, napkins. Two of everything, like the Ark. Samuel had eaten earlier in the kitchen, so this was just for her and David. Her husband never commented on how nice the table looked or said thank you for the trouble.

He would notice if she didn't do it, though. Of that she was certain. Or if there was no dinner – meat and veg and some kind of carbohydrate, nothing too spicy or too foreign – he would fly into a rage and tell her what a terrible disappointment she had been as a wife.

Not that anything like that had happened for a long time. But that was the thing with unpredictable behaviour, especially the type you got used to. While you never knew when it might happen, you always knew what a person was capable of.

Dinner that evening was lamb with asparagus, and was as unremarked upon as all the others. Barbara toyed with her food, thinking about Kate and the upcoming hearing. She hadn't told her husband about her plan to derail their daughter's attempt to get Samuel back once and for all. He wouldn't understand. Life was far more simple for him. He was happy with his golf, with his whiskey and his cronies. There was no need for her to go rocking the boat.

She could see now that he was watching her out of

the corner of his eye. He wants me to ask him what's wrong, she thought. He wants me to notice how quiet he's been the past few days. But she resisted. Let him bring it to her if he had a problem. Why should she always be the one to fix things?

David placed his knife and fork down carefully side by side on his plate. He cleared his throat and looked up at her expectantly. Barbara ignored him, staring through from the dining room to the sun room, and out into the floodlit garden beyond.

'Barb,' he said finally.

She turned to him, a quizzical look arranged on her face.

He said, 'I've been thinking –'

Oh, God! What now? Last time he'd thought they'd ended up with a hot tub, both of them too shy – or too reluctant to see each other half-naked – to ever use it.

'I've been thinking about Kate,' he said. 'And Samuel.'

Barbara speared a piece of lamb with her fork and said nothing.

'I think we should let Samuel go and live with her. I mean, right away. Not wait for this silly court case, not wait a moment longer. You've seen them together, they're getting closer every time she comes.' He folded his arms across his chest. He said, 'It's time, Barb. Time to let go.'

Barbara dropped her fork onto her plate. 'How could you be so cruel to me? Don't you care how this makes me feel?'

'This isn't about you,' he said calmly. Too calmly. This wasn't right at all. Barbara surreptitiously looked at his glass. Had he forgone his usual drink tonight? 'This is about the boy and his mother. She's changed, you must be able to see that. She's not the flighty girl we thought she was. We don't have any right to keep him away from her.'

Barbara stared at her husband. 'After everything she said about you, now you're taking her side? What the hell is going on, David?'

She could see now that he was struggling to keep his temper. For once she wanted him to lose it, wanted to have the upper hand. This calmness was more disturbing than the shouting. It wasn't like him.

He got up from the table and began to pace the dining room. 'I've been thinking about it, that's all, and the truth is ...' he stopped and turned to face her. 'Barbara, I've not been entirely blameless where Kate is concerned.'

She couldn't look at him for fear of what she might do. This is no time to get a conscience, she thought. That ship has well and truly sailed.

He carried on, pacing the room with slow, flat footsteps.

'What I mean is, there may have been a grain or two of truth in some of what she said when she left home. It's hard for me to admit this, Barbara ...'

He seemed to be accusing her, as if she were the one making it hard for him. He sat down again, pushing his plate out of the way. 'It's been weighing on my mind lately.'

'I'm not having this,' Barbara told him firmly. 'She's done something to you, made you feel guilty. It's all rubbish.'

'No!'

His voice was suddenly so loud that she glanced towards the ceiling, as though she could check on Samuel through the floorboards. It was a shock to see his sudden anger, but also there was a sighing inside her, a feeling of things falling into their proper place.

David leaned his weight on the table; she felt it tip his way slightly.

'It is not rubbish,' he bellowed. 'It's just the way things are.'

'Well, that's as maybe, but I don't see what this has to do with Samuel. He's better off here, and he always will be.'

She stood and began to pile up the plates, scraping scraps of food onto a side dish. David placed his hand on hers. His hand was hot and heavy; she could feel the tremor vibrate up her arm.

'He's better off with his mother. You're a mother – surely you know that's true. We can't keep punishing her forever, even if she is still punishing us.' He sought out her eyes, his expression challenging. 'Why are you so desperate to keep him? Are you bored, is that it? Does he give your life meaning? Or are you trying to make up for the mess you made with Katherine? Because that's what it looks like from where I'm standing.'

Whether it was his use of their daughter's full name, which neither of them had spoken since the day she left, Barbara wasn't sure, but suddenly she was suffused with her own anger, and she could not bear to look at her husband's sunken, mean-spirited face a moment longer. She shook off his hand, and then, taking up the pile of dishes, flung them with all her strength across the room.

They landed, surprisingly intact, with a hollow thud on the floor between David's stereo and the dresser. Her husband's eyes widened as she picked up each utensil in turn and threw them after the plates. A knife, followed by a fork, flew across the room in a perfect arc. And Barbara realised that she was shrieking, an incoherent stream of obscenities flowing from her mouth like water out of a dam.

So now he'd had his epiphany, after all this time. But it was too late – his crisis of conscience was one that could cost her her grandson.

She wouldn't let him ruin everything for her, not

again.

David was on his feet now, moving across the room with surprising speed and pinning her to the wall before she moved on to the crystal glasses. Which was good really, she thought absently as her husband screamed in her face, his fist as big as the leg of lamb she'd got out of the freezer earlier. Those glasses were an anniversary present from Bob and Sheila. It would have been a crime to break them.

Chapter 12

In Corrin Cove, the summer season kept everything alive, but once the tourists began to depart, the town took on a forlorn demeanour, sinking into itself as though sulking at being left suddenly alone. Yet Kate had always loved the cove best in the autumn – it felt like it belonged to her again, and the beach, with its wide expanse of sand and pebbles and the endless, uncaring sea, was her playground.

September brought with it darkening evenings when the lights across the promenade glittered like fireflies; tattered bunting dripped from shop canopies; and each and every shop on the Parade put out a sign proclaiming Sale! Everything Must Go! in red and white chest-high lettering. Kate was delighted to discover a tiny haberdasher's down by the seafront, tucked in an alley between the amusement arcade and a pizza parlour. Now her morning walk consisted of a trip down the hill, and she barely leaned on her cane at all on the way back up. Sometimes she swung the cane by her side, and it made her feel jaunty, even if only for a minute.

The date had come through for the court appearance, so now Kate knew her days of missing Sam were numbered. She had bought a calendar and a red pen with which to mark off the days as they passed. Marie saw the calendar and nodded, just once. Beyond this, her new friend had not spoken of the court case again, nor had she continued to ask questions about Evan. Instead,

Marie seemed to have thrown her energies into pairing Kate off with Patrick.

This new turn of events wasn't a complete surprise; Kate had been preoccupied, but had still seen it coming. The constant stream of information about her other lodger – that he worked out in Willows Wood as a forester; that he was amazingly good with his hands, she should see the coffee table he knocked up for Marie last Christmas; that he was only lodging here because there was a family on a long-term rental in his own house and he was too kind to kick them out of their home ... and had she mentioned that he was single and solvent and a thoroughly nice guy?

Only about a hundred times, Kate thought every time Marie launched into another one of her Patrick appreciation sessions. It was a Saturday morning, and Kate was working on an outfit she wanted to wear for the court hearing. She'd sourced a vintage pattern at the haberdasher's, along with some navy wool suiting. The pencil skirt and tailored jacket would stretch her skills, but she thought the effect would be worth it. And she could use the offcuts for Sam. Hanging on a small wooden coat hanger by her side was the sailor suit she'd made over a year ago, now too small for her son, but she planned to replicate it exactly.

'Coffee for two,' Marie called from the landing, knocking on Kate's already open door with her elbow. Kate jumped up to relieve her of one of the mugs, setting it down on top of her bookcase, far away from the delicate fabric that was laid out next to the sewing machine.

'Looks complicated.' Marie gestured to the pattern pieces Kate had already pinned in place. 'How on earth can you tell what goes where?'

Kate laughed. 'It's easy. You just follow the instructions.'

Marie picked up the sheet of paper Kate had pointed to. She dug a long fingernail into her lacquered hair to scratch at her scalp. 'Incomprehensible,' she announced. 'You, my dear, are a genius.'

'Hardly!' Kate sipped her coffee. Marie had her own espresso machine tucked away downstairs; Kate couldn't get enough of the bitter, intoxicating taste. She sighed and said, 'You know, I never liked coffee much before I was in hospital.'

'It's addictive,' Marie said, grinning.

Kate pulled a face. 'Ah well, there you go then. My mother always said I had an addictive personality.'

As Kate sipped her coffee, her gazed landed on the beautiful yellow silk curtains Marie had given her and she remembered her idea to do something nice for her friend.

'Marie, would you let me make you a dress? I've got some fabric in mind, but I was wondering what style you'd prefer.' She glanced at Marie's baggy leggings and shapeless tunic doubtfully. 'I mean, do you have anything coming up that you might need a new outfit for?'

'Oh, yes,' Marie said, giggling, 'I'm having dinner with the Queen next week, didn't I tell you?' She smiled and patted Kate's arm. 'Get away with you. Concentrate on topping up your own wardrobe and making clothes for little Sam. And getting paying customers, of course. I'm fine as I am.'

Kate only nodded. She wasn't going to be put off that easily.

'But what about Big Tony?' Kate crossed the room and fingered the silky fabric. Then she draped it across her body, twirling around until she'd wrapped herself up like a mummy. 'Ta da!' she said, laughing. 'I think he'd really like this.'

'I don't think it's Big Tony's colour,' Marie told her

seriously.

'Oh, Marie. You know what I mean. You could wear it on one of your dates. I've seen how you like to dress up for him.'

'I try, but it's mutton dressed as lamb these days.' Marie waved away Kate's protests. 'Now listen, I've got a surprise for you today. You spend too much time shut away up here like Rapunzel. It's time for you to get some fresh air into those weak little lungs of yours.'

'I go out every day,' Kate protested. 'And I'm hardly weak! I'm getting better all the time. Look, I can walk without the stick now.' She crossed the room again to demonstrate.

'And what about sleep? Every woman needs her beauty sleep. Don't think I don't know how little sleep you're getting – you could pack luggage in those bags, my dear.'

Kate tucked her chin into her neck, embarrassed. 'I have a lot on my mind,' she mumbled. 'I really don't care what I look like.'

'Beautiful women like you don't have to care,' Marie said with a sigh. 'What I wouldn't give to look so enchanting on zero sleep.'

'You said something about fresh air?' Kate reminded her, desperate to change the subject.

'Right. Patrick is going to take you out this afternoon, isn't that lovely? He's going to show you the woods where he works, give you the full guided tour. Now, don't start groaning and rolling your eyes like that – it's very unbecoming. I've made a picnic, and Patrick has taken the day off especially.'

'Marie, Patrick never works on a Saturday.'

'He does too! Not so much in the summer, but this is a busy time of year for him, so you should count yourself lucky.'

'I'm busy,' Kate said, folding her arms across her

chest. 'I can't just drop everything and go out with a man I hardly know.'

'Hardly know? You've lived under the same roof for two weeks. Kate,' she said, dropping her voice, 'he's a nice man. Take it from me, a little time spent in the company of a nice man does you the power of good.'

'But I don't want to –'

The sound of a door closing above their heads cut Kate off mid-sentence.

'He's coming,' Marie hissed. 'Act natural.'

Kate's shoulders sagged and she shook her head despairingly. Patrick descended the stairs, his footsteps ominous in the silence.

'And you might want to change into something a little more alluring than jeans and a ratty T-shirt,' Marie whispered in Kate's ear, then she winked broadly and turned to greet her other lodger.

Chapter 13

Willow Woods was a misnomer, as far as Kate could tell. She'd asked Patrick to explain the difference between a woodland and a forest, but the answer had been so complicated she wasn't sure she understood any better now than before. What she did know was, the woodlands he managed were vast and sprawling, covering much of the land between Corrin Cove and the inland villages that dotted the gently rising hills.

The journey to Willow Woods took them through a densely forested landscape, the trees folding over the narrow road to form an impenetrable canopy. By the time they reached their destination there was no sign of the bright September sun they'd left behind in Corrin Cove. Marie's picnic bounced on the back seat of Patrick's jeep, and Kate sat in silence, lamenting the fact that she hadn't been able to persuade Marie to accompany them.

'I have an appointment for a bikini wax,' Marie had announced loudly, sending Patrick rushing off downstairs, while Kate slapped her landlady on the arm for behaving so badly.

They left Patrick's jeep parked outside his 'office' – a timber structure suspended between two sturdy oaks. Kate's eyes nearly popped out of her head at the sight of it; she was even more astonished when Patrick told her he'd constructed it himself. It was utterly charming, and Kate told him so.

'You work there?' she said, shaking her head in amazement. 'But that's just ... It must be every boy's dream to grow up and have a job in a place like this.'

He grinned. 'Kind of. Come on, there's more to see.'

She followed him into the woods, glancing at his profile as they trudged side by side through the soft undergrowth. He was a handsome man, there was no denying it. There was a solidity to him, and a calmness that she thought might come from spending so much time out here, at one with nature. A sigh escaped her lips, and Patrick looked down at her, his eyebrows raised.

'Are you okay?' he said. 'It's not too much for you, is it?'

She shook her head. She had brought her cane for support, but she only intended to use it if she began to tire. They walked on in silence for a while. The quiet in here was absolute, like nothing Kate had experienced before. She could hear her own breath and her heartbeat; she was aware of every step, every crack of a twig, every snap of a branch pulled back and let go again. And she was just as aware of Patrick's breath, the rustle of his jacket, the regularity of his stride. There were no birds singing, no aeroplanes overhead, only the shushing of the wind in the trees far, far above them. You could get lost in here, she thought, and never find your way out again. If someone chose to bring you in here and leave you for dead, no one would ever find you.

Biting down an irrational surge of panic, Kate pressed on, keeping her head down so she could see only the ground in front of her. Patrick began to whistle under his breath. Kate frowned. The tune was familiar. She thought hard, trying to place it. It reminded her of childhood, of nursery rhymes and long summer days. And then she had it: the Teddy Bears' Picnic. Well, that was sort of appropriate, she supposed ...

She stopped suddenly, her eyes flashing a warning.

'What's wrong?' Patrick was ahead of her; he turned around, his expression one of mild enquiry.

'If you go down to the woods today, you're sure of a big surprise?' Kate spoke the words instead of singing them. She threw Patrick a challenging look. 'Are you trying to tell me something?'

He grinned again, a mischievous glint twinkling in his eyes. 'I wondered whether you'd pick up on that.'

'Oh, very funny.' Kate carried on walking, and Patrick fell into step beside her once more. 'So,' she said, 'do you have a big surprise for me down here in the woods?'

'I certainly do.'

She glanced up, trying to gauge his tone. 'But you're not going to tell me what it is, are you?'

'Not until we get there.'

Figured. But now she felt lighter, somehow, and the trees that closed in around them seemed to be hugging them close, keeping them safe. She allowed herself to sink into it, to try and allow all the stresses of the past few months to float away like a balloon, soon to be lost in the treetops that whispered and shivered above them.

***

'Okay, so close your eyes.'

Kate did as instructed, gripping onto her cane with one hand and Patrick's outstretched arm with the other.

'Take two steps forward. Move to your right a bit. No, the other right.'

Kate laughed. 'Sorry,' she said. 'I've never been very good with my left and my right.'

'Just as well you're not a park ranger then. Now, open your eyes.'

'Now?'

'Whenever you're ready.'

Holding on tightly, Kate opened her eyes. In front of her was a clearing, covered only with bracken and moss. She looked across at Patrick. 'It's very ... nice,' she said. 'Is this the spot you've chosen for our picnic?'

He nodded, his eyes full of amusement. 'Look up,' he whispered.

She tipped back her head, then let out a gasp, her left hand releasing Patrick and flying up to her open mouth.

'Oh, my goodness! It's incredible.' She turned to him in astonishment, then gazed back up into the trees.

High above them, swaying in the breeze as though suspended by the very air itself, was a tree house. Like the building back at the forestry centre, this was constructed from timber, but whereas Patrick's office was square and functional, the tree house was circular, mirroring the shape of the trees it nestled in so neatly, with a large round window in the side and a long rope ladder snaking down to the clearing below.

She laughed. 'Oh, you really do spend all your time out here working, don't you? Not just playing in tree houses like a little boy.'

'I work plenty,' he said, shrugging. 'Well, okay, maybe there's a bit of the boy left in me still. But all work and no play makes you dull, right? Like you, stuck at that sewing machine all day long. I was glad when Marie said you wanted to come out here and see the woods.'

'She said I wanted –?' Kate bit off her words and met Patrick's gaze. 'Is that what Marie said?'

He nodded, then sighed. 'Ah, I see. Marie has played us both, it seems.'

'Right.' Kate looked at her feet, swallowing down a nugget of disappointment. So he'd only offered to bring her because Marie asked him, not because he wanted to.

'She did make us this picnic,' he said, hoisting the

basket up onto his shoulder. 'So we shouldn't be too cross with her.'

Kate shook her head, not quite trusting herself to speak.

'Come on then,' Patrick said. 'You won't believe the view from up there.'

But Kate held back, eyeing the ladder doubtfully. 'Patrick, I can't climb that. There's no way I can do it, and not just because of this.' She lifted her cane. 'I wouldn't have been able to climb a rope ladder when I was fit and well.'

He shook his head, still smiling. 'That's just there for emergencies. And for when I feel like challenging myself a little. Come on – there are steps on the other side of those trees.'

She followed him, biting her lip, overwhelmed at the thought of being high in the treetops with this man who seemed at once so gentle but at the same time strong and capable.

They rounded a giant trunk at least three metres in circumference, and there, embedded in the tree at regular intervals, was a set of wooden steps, each tread only just wide enough to stand on. The treads wound around the trunk, up and up, accompanied by a thick rope handrail, leading to a timber walkway that had been hidden from their vantage point back in the clearing. Patrick laid the picnic basket on the woodland floor and gestured to Kate to go first.

'You'll be fine, Kate,' he told her. 'They're just spiral stairs like you'd find in any castle turret or stately home. Try to forget that you're outside, and lean into the body of the tree. Oh, and don't look down.' He grinned at her and nodded again for her to move. 'I'll be right behind you. I won't let you fall.'

She took a deep breath, then began to climb. 'I don't actually like stately homes,' she told him over her shoulder.

'I didn't think so,' he said, chuckling.

'I'm more of an outdoors kind of a girl.'

'Right. That's what I thought.'

'In fact, I'd like to live in the woods, just me and Sam, just escape from the world, never have to bother with anyone, ever.'

She was babbling now, talking for the sake of it. Patrick kept up his own chatter behind her, egging her on, telling her she was doing great. The truth was, she'd never been an outdoors kind of person at all. She'd spent her teenage years resenting Corrin Cove – hadn't even heard of these woods until today, despite growing up a stone's throw from them. She'd spent all of her adult years until now in a sprawling metropolis, where the only greenery had been the odd patch of municipal grass. She climbed on, not daring to look at anything other than the next tread in front of her, trying not to think about the distance from here to the ground.

And then she was at the top, stepping onto a sturdy platform of solid timber and gripping hold of the handrail exultantly. 'I made it!' she cried.

'You certainly did.' Patrick stepped up from the tree-stairway behind her, for a moment so close she could feel the entire length of his body pressed against her. She closed her eyes, fighting the desire to lean into him, to enjoy the view while encircled in his arms – she knew she would fit so snugly there. Too soon he moved on to stand by her side, and Kate let out a tiny sigh and opened her eyes.

'Wow,' she exclaimed. 'It really is incredible.'

Up here she could see the curve of the forested land, see how it fell away down towards the cove. She gazed across the treetops, shaking her head in amazement.

'It looks like rain,' she said, peering out towards the ocean. Darkening clouds were flattened against the sea, the sky an angry violet above them. But Patrick was already crossing the narrow walkway, half turned and holding out his hand for her to join him.

She followed Patrick across the walkway into the tree house, enjoying the sensation of being on top of the world. While Patrick went to fetch the picnic, shimmying down the rope ladder with ease, Kate stood at the round window and closed her eyes again, allowing the rising breeze to cool her face and lift her hair, feeling so alive, so animated, she wanted to capture the moment and keep it with her for all time. She imagined bringing Sam up here, and decided to ask Patrick if he thought it would be safe.

They ate their picnic in silence, but the silence was companionable, and Kate felt as though she had known Patrick all her life. She was glad he didn't bombard her with questions the way Marie did; she only wanted to savour the moment.

'I suppose we should be going,' Patrick said after they'd wolfed down all of Marie's sandwiches and posh crisps and home-baked sausage rolls. 'I heard you tell Marie you were busy. I don't want to take up too much of your day.'

'Can't we stay just a little longer?' Kate heard herself asking. 'I mean, only if you can spare the time.' She swallowed, aware all over again of the effect his proximity had on her. 'It's just that it took so much effort to get up here in the first place – it seems a shame to go back so soon. Maybe we could just ... sit for a while?'

Patrick nodded, then settled back against the side of the tree house and closed his eyes. Kate studied him for a while, tracing the faint lines on his face with an imaginary finger, wondering what he was thinking, what secrets he kept, what he thought about her. She snuggled deeper into the blankets that lined the floor, and leaned back against one of the giant cushions. The tree house rocked gently, and Kate felt like a baby in a cradle, swaying, safe, up here on the top of the world.

'Kate?'

She awoke with a start to find Patrick leaning over her. He was smiling, but the smile was strained. She looked around, disorientated.

'I must have fallen asleep,' she told him, rubbing her eyes with the heels of her hands.

'You haven't been asleep for long, but the storm came over really quickly.'

'Storm?' she said, but already she was becoming aware of the pelting rain on the roof of the tree house, the water lashing in through the window, the violent rocking of the tree tops. 'Oh, my God. Are we okay up here?'

Patrick didn't answer. He was pulling at the blankets, searching for something. The light had all but gone, although it couldn't be more than three or four o'clock, and everything inside the tree house looked rubbed out and blurry. Kate shook her head, trying to clear it.

'Did you fall asleep too?' she asked him. 'What time is it?'

'We need to get back to the car,' he said. 'We don't want to get stuck out here in a storm.'

'Why? I mean, it'll be okay, won't it? It'll blow over.'

He stood up, holding two blankets and a torch. His face was deadly serious. 'Kate, you do not want to be stuck on top of a tree in the middle of a lightning storm. Now, it's getting dark, it's absolutely hammering it down out there, and the storm is getting closer. We need to get you down, and fast. Those steps are going to be slippery as hell, and it's harder going down than up, even in good conditions. It's even harder when the light starts to go.'

'Oh.' Kate swallowed and looked out at the

darkening sky. He was right. The climb down would be treacherous, especially for someone whose legs were already tired and not used to such strenuous activity. She stood up gingerly, wincing at the stiffness in her thighs. Patrick watched her, his expression grave. A blast of icy rain blew in through the window and hit her in the face. She reeled back, catching her breath.

'It's my fault,' she said, wiping her face on her sleeve.

Patrick turned to the doorway, gesturing for her to follow. 'No, it isn't. Right, when we get outside you're going to be soaked quite quickly, so here's the plan–'

'I saw the storm coming.' She had to shout above the wind now to make herself heard. 'Earlier, when we first came up here. I saw the cloud formation coming in over the sea. I know the signs, Patrick. I grew up here.' She shook her head angrily. 'I should have said something.'

'Kate, it's weather. There's nothing we can do about the–'

A sudden flash and an almighty crash of thunder sent them both reeling back inside the tree house. Kate blinked; she could only see red, then black, then her vision began to clear.

'Did you see that?' Patrick shouted.

'What was it?'

'The lightning. I think it hit the staircase. Hang on.'

'Wait!'

Kate reached out after him, but Patrick was already running across the walkway. Kate stood in the doorway, sheltered from the driving rain, and watched him check the other supporting tree. He ran back, already drenched to the skin.

'It's no good,' he said, stepping inside the wooden structure and shaking off the water like a wet dog. 'The lightning strike has split the trunk. There's no way we can get down that way.'

Kate stared at him, open-mouthed. Patrick sighed, his

chest heaving. 'Kate, you're going to have to go down the ladder.'

***

'Are you ready?'

'As I'll ever be,' Kate whispered. There was no one to hear her; Patrick had gone down first. His parting words – 'All the better to catch you if you fall' – had hardly been reassuring. He shouted up again now, but his voice was lost to the wind. Kate shivered, then moved her hands and feet in unison, the way Patrick had shown her, and began to descend.

She could feel him trying to brace the rope ladder from below, trying to keep it as stable as possible, but it was in the middle that it began to lurch wildly backwards and forwards, and here she began to lose her resolve. It was impossible. Her hands were frozen and wet and slippery; water was running down from her soaking hair into her eyes; every muscle in her body was shaking with effort.

Somehow she kept on moving her hands and her feet, downwards, onwards, and then, suddenly, she was at the bottom, her feet hitting the ground, the wonderful stable ground, her body falling limply into Patrick's waiting arms. He held her close for a moment, steadying her, his breath warm in her hair. Then he held her away from him and peered into her eyes.

'Are you okay?'

She nodded. She really didn't think she could speak.

'Oh, my God, Kate. Well done. You were amazing.'

'Thanks,' she whispered. It was nothing, she thought. You should try learning to walk again.

'Come on,' Patrick said, slipping his hand into hers. 'Let's get you home.'

They half ran back to the jeep, Patrick navigating the

way through the trees. 'I know these woods better than I know myself,' he told her, and Kate smiled at this. When they arrived back at the jeep, he helped her into her seat, treating her like a precious cargo. Then he ran around to the driver's side and jumped in.

He looked across at her and grinned.

'Not bad for an afternoon out,' he said. 'Do I know how to show a girl a good time or what?'

'You certainly do,' Kate answered weakly. 'You sure gave me a big surprise.'

'Here, put this over you. It will stop you getting a chill.' He took the spare blanket out of a carrier bag and leaned over to wrap it around her. She turned. Their faces were inches apart.

'Patrick,' she said, 'I ...'

He put his finger on her lips, then traced the curve of her cheek, brushing her wet hair out of her face, squeezing some of the water out of it with the corner of the blanket.

'I'm sorry,' he whispered. 'For ruining our afternoon.'

He was so close Kate could feel his breath on her cheek, could see only his mouth, could hear only his voice. 'I thought we couldn't help the weather,' she murmured.

'True.'

Kate held her breath. The moment stretched out, frozen. And then Patrick leaned in and touched his lips to hers.

'Thank you for a lovely day, Kate,' he said. He met her eyes, then he moved back and started the engine.

Kate gripped the blanket close to her as they set off down the rutted track and headed out of the woods. It smelt of Patrick.

The rain had eased a little, but the track was muddy and the headlights picked out fallen branches and wide flooded depressions, and once a scampering rabbit, confused and far from home.

'Marie will be wondering what we've been up to all this time, won't she?' Patrick said once they were clear of the woodland track.

Kate let out a groan. She really didn't feel like Marie's special brand of inquisition right now.

'Don't worry,' Patrick said, bouncing the jeep around a corner. 'I'll just tell her that we slept together and then I saved your life. That should shut her up.'

Kate smiled and closed her eyes. Yes, she thought. It probably would.

But when they arrived back at the house on Bow Hill, Marie wasn't waiting with an expectant expression, demanding to know where they'd been all day, eager for the gory details. Instead, she was standing in the hallway, looking for all the world as though she'd been standing there half the afternoon.

'Kate,' she said, her voice small and apologetic. 'I'm so sorry.'

'What is it?' Kate rushed to her friend and grabbed both of her hands. She thought of Sam, only Sam. Please God, don't let anything have happened to Sam.

'There's a man here,' Marie said, her face crumpling with anxiety. 'He's waiting for you in your room. I shouldn't have let him in, it was so stupid. But he said he was your friend, he said you were expecting him. Well, of course, I knew you weren't or you would have said. I mean, you would have, wouldn't you? If you were expecting someone?'

Kate could feel Patrick behind her. She had the feeling he was braced, ready to prop her up again at any moment. She focused on Marie, trying all the while to calm her thoughts. No, she thought. Please don't let it be him.

But she knew, before Marie spoke his name, that her worst nightmare was already a reality.

'He said he was Sam's dad, Kate. He said you would want to see him. It's Evan. I'm so sorry.'

Chapter 14

Barbara stood at the drawing room window and watched the car pull into her driveway. She looked at her watch, then back at the car. It wasn't a taxi, but some kind of utility vehicle. A jeep, perhaps? Kate must have got a lift from someone, no doubt the man Evan had mentioned earlier. Although Barbara had known this was coming she didn't feel prepared for it one bit. In the downstairs cloakroom she had just enough time to reapply her lipstick before the doorbell rang with its up and down tune. She raised her eyes to the ceiling, then went to let her daughter in.

Evan, Barbara was beginning to realise, was a bit of a liability.

'I didn't know it was supposed to be a secret,' he'd said when he turned up on her doorstep that morning, looking her up and down appraisingly and laughing at her concern. She'd only just managed to usher him into the garage before David came downstairs for breakfast.

No, thought Barbara, neither did I exactly. But she hadn't expected Kate to find out so soon either, and the fact that Evan had taken it upon himself to simply turn up at Kate's and announce his presence had left her feeling sidelined. This was her plan, not Evan's, and she, Barbara, was supposed to be calling the shots. But then she imagined Kate holed up in her grotty bedsit – Evan said it was a real dump of a place with paint peeling off the window frames and no central heating – and the image gave Barbara a faint buzz of pleasure. More ammunition for her case. He also said that Kate had no idea what he was doing here, only that Barbara had contacted him 'for Sam's benefit'.

Which was something, she supposed.

After sending Evan off with strict instructions to talk to no one else, Barbara had steeled herself for her daughter's inevitable visit. She regarded Kate now with wariness, noticing that she was no longer leaning so heavily on the stick that Barbara found so disconcerting. She was getting better, getting stronger.

As they moved into the hall, Barbara could sense Kate scanning the house for Sam. 'He's on a play date,' she said, not bothering to turn around. Kate said nothing.

In the dining room they took seats facing each other across the polished furniture. Barbara smoothed down her skirt, unable to keep her hands still. She noticed a patch of dust on the bookcase by the window; she must have missed it earlier. It was no wonder, really. Not when she had all this going on.

'I must say, you've surpassed yourself this time, Mother. That was a master stroke indeed. You must feel very proud.'

Barbara flinched at her daughter's voice. The level of disgust was unmistakable. 'I don't know what you're talking about,' she countered. She fingered the antimacassar on the arm of the chair, shifting it slightly so the pattern matched that of the chair fabric perfectly.

'It won't work,' Kate said. 'Whatever plan you've got for Evan, you've bitten off more than you can chew.'

'Oh, spare me the clichés. I contacted Sam's father – what possible harm could that do?'

'You know what kind of a person he is. You wouldn't have done it if you didn't think there'd be some benefit in it for you. Are you going to try and get him on your side? Get him to stand up in court and say he thinks Sam would be better off with his grandparents instead of me? Is that your plan?'

'It's none of your business what Evan and I have discussed,' Barbara said. 'Or with whom he thinks Samuel should live.'

'It's none of his business, you mean,' Kate corrected. 'Mum, he has a criminal record. You do realise that, don't you? If Evan is your trump card then you are going to be sorely disappointed.'

'Is that all?' Barbara looked at her watch. 'Well, if you don't mind I need to put lunch on.'

'Did you not think of me at all?' Kate leaned forward, her head tilted to the side. 'When you came to stay with me I told you all about Evan. I told you what he was capable of. How could you have brought him back into our lives like this? Back into Sam's life?'

'You know as well as I do the cards are stacked in your favour. Yes, the court will listen to the child's mother, but it will give equal weight to the wishes of his father. What choice did I have?'

Kate stood up, making Barbara squint to see her face. 'You could have just worked it out with me instead of keeping me away from Sam. We could have had joint care of him for a while. There were lots of options open to you. You could have done what was right, what was best for him in the long run.'

'And let you win? Not a chance.' Barbara kept her back straight. She would retain her dignity throughout this ordeal no matter what her daughter did or said. No doubt the hysterics would start soon, the whole thing reduced to an emotional circus. She was certainly her father's daughter.

But Kate only looked at Barbara levelly and said, 'It is not a game. There are no winners and losers here. Only a child without his mother, and a mother who is sorry for the mistakes she made in the past and who wants to put them right. A mother who needs to be with her son.' And then she folded her hands in her lap and turned her gaze to the window.

Barbara thought for a moment. This new Kate was bothering her. She had expected rages and tears and accusations – and she was prepared to defend herself against them. She had nothing to offer up to this calm judgment. The silence settled over them like a thick, suffocating blanket. Barbara looked at her watch again.

'Tell me,' Kate said suddenly, her voice barely more than a whisper, 'was finding Evan Dad's idea? Did he put you up to it?'

For a second or two Barbara considered letting David take the blame. But what was the point? In less than three weeks they would be in court, and Barbara needed to keep her daughter as rattled as possible.

'No,' she said triumphantly. 'It has nothing whatsoever to do with him. In fact, your father is all for you having Samuel back. He doesn't want him here with us, he never really has. Says we should give Samuel back to you, as though he's a lawnmower we borrowed for the weekend.'

Barbara forced herself to stand, heading for the kitchen. Her daughter followed. Barbara could feel eyes boring into her back. 'What?' she snapped, swinging around, her face suddenly twisted with rage. 'What do you want from me?'

'You know,' Kate said, walking to the breakfast bar and perching her small frame on a stool, 'there was a time when I would have answered that question by saying I wanted you to be a normal mother, to care enough about me to take some action. Now – now I wouldn't bother. There's nothing normal about you, is there? Just something very, very sad.'

Barbara ground her teeth in fury. 'How dare you! How dare you insult me in my own home. There is nothing wrong with me that having a decent, respectful daughter wouldn't cure.'

'You're probably right, Mum. But whose fault is that? I didn't ask to be brought up in this environment. I didn't ask to have a violent drunk as a father, and an emotionally distant mother. But I got them anyway.'

'How you can sit there and make those accusations about your father is beyond me. It's all in your head, always has been.'

A fragment of memory tugged at Barbara's mind – a picture of her daughter at Samuel's age, wobbling down the stairs and calling for her mummy, her hair stuck up on the top of her head as though she'd been pulled by it ...

She shoved the memory aside and felt her way to the sink, clinging to it blindly. Kate's voice came at her, relentless.

'You've always been in denial about it. Even now, after all this time, you just can't admit that he was a violent man. Even though you know I saw him hit you dozens of times. I remember you going to hospital. And you know he lost his temper with me, too. But you did nothing. Is that why you won't accept it? Because you feel guilty?'

Her daughter paused, but Barbara wouldn't answer. She ran cold water over her wrists. Her head was pounding. It was becoming harder and harder to think clearly. And all the while Kate's voice droned on.

'He used to come up to my room sometimes, after you two had had one of your fights. He used to sit there and cry. I could smell the alcohol, but I had no idea what it was. If I made a noise or said the wrong thing he'd grab my hair and slap my face so hard I would see stars. I thought they were real stars – for years I was frightened of the night sky. Once he told me that if I didn't stop crying he'd hold me upside down over the stairs and drop me, and that my head would be squashed inside my body for ever. But I hadn't even made a noise. And you – you did nothing. Later I came to you, when he'd gone to bed or passed out or something, I came to you for reassurance. I was so frightened. Do you know what you said? Do you remember?'

Barbara's head was going to explode. She rounded on Kate and screamed, 'Get out of my house. Get out, get out, you evil child.'

Her daughter didn't flinch. Instead she shook her head slowly.

'No, Mother. What you actually said was, "You must have been asking for it, Katherine". That was how you comforted me, that was how you protected your own daughter. So when you ask yourself now why I turned out the way I did, so ungrateful and so useless, living with a low-life like Evan all those years, you just remember that. And if you're still wondering why I'm determined not to leave my son with you for a second longer than necessary, then think on this – it's not just my father I can't trust. It's you as well. Sam isn't safe with either of you, and make no mistake – I won't rest until I get him back.'

For a second or two it was quiet, and Barbara breathed in the silent air, relishing it, letting it wash over her. Then the front door slammed so violently it rattled the pans on the shelf above her head. No! Barbara thought. I can't let her go like this. She raced out after Kate, finding her already inside the strange car, backing out of the driveway. Frantically, Barbara rapped on the passenger window, signalling for Kate to wind it down. Her daughter looked up at her, her face a mask of disgust.

As the car sped away along the lane, Barbara sank to the ground and covered her face with her hands. The gravel was sharp at her knees and pierced her tights, drawing blood. She wept, soundlessly and without thinking, only aware of the pain in her heart and the pounding fear that beat at her mind like a pulse.

Chapter 15

'I think there's a girl in here who needs caffeine.'

Kate looked up from her sewing machine and offered Marie a weak smile. 'You might be right,' she said, stretching out the tension in her neck.

Marie set the mugs down on the windowsill, then lowered herself onto Kate's single bed – the only place in the room to sit, if you didn't count the two rickety chairs at the dining-stroke-sewing table.

'How are you bearing up, kiddo?'

Kate let out a heavy sigh. 'I've been better. Just when I thought things were looking positive, first Evan turns up, and then I have a massive row with my mother.' She shook her head, her eyes brimming with unwanted tears. 'I don't know, Marie. Sometimes I wonder if my mother isn't actually a bit crazy. The way she looks at me, the vitriol in her voice. She really, really hates me.'

'She can't hate you, she's your mother. I might not have kids, but I know that much. Mums don't hate their daughters, no matter what.'

'Well, what is it, then?' Kate asked, turning to face her friend. 'I wish someone would explain it to me. I can understand that she's become attached to Sam, and I can understand her being anxious at first, wondering if I was well enough to look after him, worried she might lose touch with me – and him – again. But yesterday ... Ah, Marie. You'd have to have been there. She is one twisted woman.'

'And she didn't deny that it was her who contacted Evan? The story he told you was true?'

Kate nodded.

Marie let out a low whistle. 'Wow, that's cold. Going to all that trouble, tracking him down through social media and goodness knows what else – she must have been really desperate to find him.'

'He said he was in Scotland, had been working there for a while. Said he knew nothing of the accident – that's what he called it, an accident. He flew down, apparently, as soon as he got her message.' Kate laughed bitterly. 'I bet she even sent him the money for the air fare.'

'What's in it for her?' Marie wondered aloud. 'I mean, how does she know he won't side with you?'

'Evan will go where the money is,' Kate said, turning down the corners of her mouth. 'If I had a big enough bank balance I might be in with a chance, but as it is –'

'Your mother will be pulling his strings,' Marie finished. 'Yes, I see.' She regarded Kate thoughtfully. Kate could see her friend's mind working overtime, and the next thing out of her mouth wasn't a total surprise.

'Although,' Marie said, 'you might have more to bargain with than you think. It seemed to me like he was very, very pleased to see you at the weekend, what with you looking so great and all – if a little soggy – and I was thinking –'

'Don't, Marie.' Kate held up her hand, cutting her off. 'Don't even go there. It is absolutely not going to happen.'

'Not even for Sam?'

'That is not fair! And no, not even for Sam. Fine, I've said it. Because it wouldn't be for Sam, would it? It would be to fight against her, and I'm not turning this into a fight. This is about what's right, Marie. I have to keep hold of that. Don't you understand? I'll be lost otherwise.'

Marie crossed the small room and gave Kate a hug. 'You're right,' she said, 'and I'm sorry for even thinking it. Now, let's talk about something else. Did you and Patrick have a nice time on Saturday? I hope the weather didn't spoil it for you.'

'I wouldn't say spoil it exactly ...' Kate felt her body heating up as she remembered the race through the woods, Patrick's lips on hers, his warm hands on her cold, wet skin. She had felt like a teenager again. She had felt alive.

'Come on, out with it. You were glowing when you walked in, both of you. I saw the look on your face, before you heard about Evan the terrible.'

Kate shrugged. 'He showed me his tree house.'

'Did he now?' Marie let out a loud guffaw and nudged Kate in the ribs. 'Impressive, was it?'

'That wasn't a euphemism! He has a tree house in the woods. We had our picnic there.'

'I know, I was just teasing. So, come on – let's have the rest of it. Did you get on okay? Was he the perfect gentleman? Don't keep me in suspense.'

Kate gave Marie a brief account of their trip to the woods, growing pink in the face when she got to the part about falling asleep after lunch. 'It was your fault,' she said, 'for making such a massive picnic.'

Marie smiled, her eyes twinkling. 'I see. And that was it? You just "fell asleep"?'

'Don't say it like that, as though it's some kind of code. Yes, that was it. And then, well ... You know the rest. There was a storm, we got wet. End of story.'

'Which is why you were both so flushed when you got back,' Marie said, smiling.

Kate nodded. 'The buildings he's made out there are incredible. He's very talented.'

'And good with his hands, I'll bet,' Marie said dreamily.

'Whatever.' Kate sipped her coffee, trying to push the images of Patrick being good with his hands in all sorts of interesting ways out of her mind.

'He likes you,' Marie said, winking. 'Look how he rushed to your rescue on Saturday. He practically threw Evan out of the house.'

Kate grimaced at the memory. She hadn't known what to do, how to face Evan after all this time. And when she'd walked into her room and seen him standing there, holding Sam's little sailor suit and giving her that same old come-hither smile, his eyes the same eyes she'd gazed into for years and his body lean and compact, giving off his own personal brand of undeniable appeal ... She had been lost then, racing back across the years, full of anger and confusion and bitter regret, unable to pull a single coherent thought out of her mind.

Evan had the better of her, as usual. 'Why, Kate,' he'd said, 'you look amazing. Your mum told me you'd been in hospital, some kind of accident? But look at you! Radiant as always, and with your own little entourage of adoring fans, of course.'

This comment was aimed at Patrick and Marie, who had followed her into her room. Kate could see that Evan expected her to tell them to go, that he wanted this reunion to be private and on his own terms, but there was no way that was going to happen. It was only when he started talking about her mother, and how she'd dragged him down from Scotland that Kate had begun to react. And then the shaking had started so badly she could hardly stand up.

'What's wrong with you?' Evan said, genuinely puzzled. He'd looked at Patrick, his expression measuring, and directed his next question to him. 'So what's your story, mate?'

Patrick's expression darkened even further; he turned to Kate, his eyebrows raised. What do you want me to do? he seemed to be asking, but Kate was still shaking – she couldn't think straight. She just wanted Evan to go away and leave her alone. She watched him, tracking his steps as he paced the room, picking up her things, putting them down. It was inconceivable that he was here, now. He belonged in Manchester, in the underbelly of a city, surrounded by high, blackened buildings and a small patch of sky. Not in Corrin Cove, standing by the dusty window with the sun turning his white-blonde hair yellow and highlighting the sharpness of his cheekbones, the blueness of his eyes.

'You can run along now,' he said to Patrick and Marie, and he accompanied this with a little swishing motion of his hands. 'Me and Kate want a bit of time on our own.'

'No!' She heard the word, and only then realised it was she who had spoken. Suddenly the spell was broken, and she was on her feet, bearing down on him, all the anger and resentment of the past few years spilling out of her broken heart.

That Patrick had ended up escorting Evan out of the house, possibly for Evan's sake as much as her own, was still a source of embarrassment for Kate. And what happened outside her mother's house was even worse.

'I shouldn't have let Patrick give me a lift to Woodland Cottage,' she said now, chewing on her bottom lip. 'It was just awful, my mum running out like that. What must he think of me?'

She shouldn't care, but she did.

Marie shook her head, patting Kate's shoulder consolingly. 'No doubt he thinks you're human, just like everyone else. And perhaps that you have a very odd family,' she conceded. 'But then, who doesn't? Look at me and Big Tony! My family think I'm insane to be dating him again. But I tell them, he's my first love. I've never been able to resist him – why should it be any different now?'

Kate smiled. She'd yet to meet Big Tony, but she couldn't help liking the sound of him – Marie's down-to-earth enthusiasm was infectious. She glanced at her watch, then jumped up in alarm.

'Marie, I can't stand here talking all day – I've got an appointment with Elizabeth in half an hour.'

Marie gathered up the coffee cups and headed for the door. 'Do you want me to come with you?' she offered. 'A bit of moral support?'

'Thanks, but it's only Elizabeth – I don't think it will be too onerous.'

***

'She said what?'

Kate reeled back in her chair as though struck by an invisible hand. Elizabeth frowned, then shook her head.

'I'm sorry, Kate. There's nothing I can do. She said you can see him, but only at a neutral location. I thought the children's centre here in Corrin Cove would be best – it's fun for Samuel, and the staff are used to this kind of thing.'

'They're used to this kind of thing?' Kate widened her eyes, incredulous. 'They're used to grandparents preventing a child's own mother from visiting him in his own home? After that child's mother was unable to look after him because she was in a coma after being attacked in her own home?' Her voice grew louder with each word, her face growing redder and hotter as the blood pounded in her head. 'Elizabeth, am I the only sane person around here? Can no one else see that this is wrong!' She slammed her fist down on the table. Their coffee cups clattered in their saucers; a nearby customer glanced over, then resumed his conversation. 'And,' Kate added, her teeth clenched together so hard she could feel them grinding, 'his name is not Samuel! It's Sam. Just Sam.'

Kate tried to calm her breathing. Elizabeth sat impassively, her expression unreadable.

'My mother,' Kate said slowly, 'is treating me like I'm a danger to Sam, like I'm someone so unstable she's afraid to have me in her house. But it's her who's unstable. Can't you see that?'

Still Elizabeth said nothing. Kate tapped her fingers on the table, her thoughts flying around her mind like angry wasps, every memory a sharp sting in the tail.

'You know,' she said, 'this is all because of those drugs that were found in the flat. I'm right, aren't I? My mother whipped Sam away from Manchester within a matter of weeks, and social services didn't do anything to stop her. You cheered her on, helping her get the guardianship order, never once thinking what it would mean to me when I woke up.' She noticed Elizabeth's expression and laughed. 'Oh, well, I don't suppose anyone expected me to wake up, did they? But I did, and here I am – how inconvenient for everyone. The police would have arrested me if they thought there was any real evidence against me, but clearly they don't. Why do you think that is?'

'I suppose, as you say, there wasn't enough evidence to press charges,' Elizabeth agreed.

'Right, exactly. And that's because in actual fact there wasn't any evidence to link me to the drugs because I had nothing to do with them being there. Someone must have planted them.' Kate's eyes narrowed suddenly. She sat up straighter and clasped her hands together. 'You know, I have an idea who might have done it.'

'Who?' Elizabeth said tiredly.

'My mother! Don't you see? It all makes sense. She must have taken my key while I was in hospital and snuck in and planted the drugs in the toilet cistern herself. She'd planned to get Sam away from me all along, even when she came to stay earlier in the year. She never thought I was good enough to be a mum, has never forgiven me for what I said about my father when I left home. Oh, it all makes sense now. That's why she's been so upset since I came back – and that's why she never came to visit, even after I woke up and started to get better.'

'The police found them when they searched your flat directly after you were attacked,' Elizabeth pointed out. 'So your mother couldn't have stolen your keys and hidden them there herself.'

'She might have done it when she was staying with me, though. I wouldn't have noticed. The stuff could have been there for months.'

'No, it couldn't. The police report said that the landlord had to fix the toilet only a month before the break-in. There was nothing hidden there. He would have noticed.'

'Well, fine. But that doesn't mean it wasn't her.'

'And how precisely do you imagine your mother got her hands on three bags of cannabis resin, Kate? In Manchester, while looking after Sam and visiting you in hospital?'

Kate shrugged. 'She's clearly a resourceful woman. She found Evan, didn't she? That's not an easy thing to do.'

Elizabeth gathered together her phone and keys, then sat back and faced Kate squarely. 'I think this new arrangement will be better for you and Sam. The children's centre is a great environment, and you won't have to keep rubbing up against your parents. You'll see him there three times a week – I'll come along the first time, show you the lie of the land. It won't be for long. You know that.'

'I have a bad feeling about Evan,' Kate said, leaning

low across the table and dropping her voice. 'Did my mother say anything to you about him when she phoned?'

'Not one word.' The social worker stood up; their meeting was over. Kate rose and followed her to the door of the café.

'Is she letting him see Sam, do you think?' That would be the worst kind of insult. Not that Kate imagined Evan would be bothered about seeing his son anyway.

Elizabeth shrugged. 'Look, I'm doing all I can. The only thing you can do now is dig in and wait for the court date. Sooner or later your mother will have to come to terms over this. What you decide to do then – about Sam's dad or your parents – will be up to you.'

Kate flopped down onto a wrought iron bench outside the café and watched Elizabeth drive away. After a while she got up again, but found she couldn't face returning to Bow Hill yet. Instead, she headed for the beach. She would sit for a while and gaze out to sea, the way she had all those years ago whenever she felt overwhelmed or saw that the world didn't understand her. Those teenage concerns seemed so small now, so insignificant, and Kate longed to go back to a simpler time – even just a year ago, when all she'd had to think about was where the next meal was coming from and whether she'd be able to afford her rent. Or whether she'd ever be able to sleep through the night again.

She laughed to herself: a bitter, unhappy sound. Be careful what you wish for. There she had been, struggling with a baby, wishing someone would just let her sleep. She'd have liked to have slept for a week. She'd been given the best part of a year. And then she'd woken up to find that her whole world had been turned upside down while she slept on, helpless and unaware.

At the edge of the beach she took off her trainers and socks and walked across the compacted sand to where the sea curled back in on itself in a swelling, sucking, continuous motion. The water was icy on her toes, but after a while she got used to it. She turned up her jeans and waded in to her shins. She stretched out her arms, not caring who saw her, not caring at all. And she allowed the sound of the sea to fill her ears, drowning out all her bitter thoughts, at least for a while.

Chapter 16

The two hours Kate spent at the children's centre with Sam were, as Elizabeth had predicted, stress-free and fun. There was a stay-and-play session in progress, and Kate enjoyed being just another mum spending time with her toddler, stepping in from time to time to negotiate the sharing of a toy, feeling joy whenever her boy came running to her for help or reassurance. But whereas all the other parents would get to take their offspring home at the end of the session, Kate had to walk away and leave Sam with Elizabeth, who would be overseeing the handover back to Kate's mother.

As far as the other mums were concerned, Kate was just like them, and she was glad of the anonymity. There was one awkward moment when Kate recognised someone she'd gone to school with, a girl called Denise who was now the mother of twin baby girls and a rowdy boy of four, but the woman was so harassed she barely gave Kate a second glance. Kate knew she was practically unrecognisable as the Katherine who had left Corrin Cove at eighteen. She was much thinner now, her hair longer and darker. Life had left its mark on her face – the years spent partying and eating too little and worrying about what Evan was up to had made her drawn around the eyes, her skin pale with fine lines on her forehead. Denise had fared far better, Kate noticed. Blooming with health and vitality, the girl had blossomed into a beautiful woman, and her clothing and manicured nails spoke of an enviously affluent lifestyle.

Kate spent as much time as she could simply gazing at Sam, drinking him in, reaching out to touch his back, his arms, his chunky little legs whenever he toddled past her.

'It's like you haven't seen him for weeks,' one of the mothers remarked, laughing when Kate swept Sam off his feet and held his soft cheek to hers.

You have no idea, Kate thought.

Too soon, the session was over, and Kate said a tearful goodbye to Sam, who regarded her thoughtfully, clinging onto her skirt with both fists.

'Bye bye,' he said, staring up into her face. 'Bye bye, Mummy.'

Kate walked away, her hand over her mouth, trying to contain all the joy and the pain that threatened to spill over. He had called her Mummy. She wanted to shout it to the world; she wanted to dance and jump with pure pleasure, even while her heart was breaking at having to leave him all over again.

Out in the street, she started to walk in the direction of Bow Hill. A black car, low and gleaming, pulled up alongside her. A man's voice called her name. She stopped and glanced to her side.

Grinning at her from the driver's seat, one tanned arm leaning out of the window, was Evan.

'Give you a lift somewhere?' he enquired mildly.

Kate fought the urge to run. It was ridiculous: this was Evan. He was Sam's father, and although he'd hurt her deeply many, many times, there was no need for her to feel so repelled at the sight of him. Kate had to admit it was partly because she was afraid of her own reactions. He had always been able to charm her, just like Big Tony charmed Marie. One twist of that mobile mouth of his, one flash of those blue eyes, and she was putty in his hands.

Not anymore. She was determined not to fall for it

again, even if it would help her to get Sam back. She would be cool and polite, not shivering and emotional, and then Evan would see that she was over him once and for all.

'Sure,' she said, smiling blandly. She walked around to the passenger door, noticing that Evan didn't leap out of the car to open it the way Patrick would have. Patrick was worth ten of Evan, and the thought gave her a frisson of excitement. She hugged it to herself, and hid it away to think about later. Right now she had an ex to deal with.

***

Evan didn't drive her straight back to Bow Hill, but Kate wasn't surprised at this. She recognised that he needed to talk to her and found she didn't begrudge him that. It would be good to clear the air. Plus she wanted to find out what her mother was up to.

Whether or not she could trust Evan to tell her the truth was another matter.

He headed out on the south road, and for a while she watched the ocean churn and boil below them, smelling the salt on the air, feeling oddly calm. He asked if she'd eaten lunch yet, and only nodded when she told him she wasn't hungry. There was a tea room up on the cliff not far away, and Kate was surprised to find herself suggesting they stopped there for a drink. Evan nodded again, then steered off the main road and began to round the head of the bay.

'Evan,' Kate said smoothly, glad to hear that her voice was in check, 'I'd really like to know what you're doing here. I mean, what you're really doing here.'

'Well, because you asked so nicely, I'll tell you,' he said, smiling across at her. 'You really do look lovely, you know. Although I think being in a coma is taking beauty sleep a bit too far.'

Kate smiled in spite of herself. 'I'm glad you can joke about it, Evan. It hasn't been much fun for me. Especially waking up and finding out that my own mother has stolen my son.'

He glanced at her again; she could feel his eyes on her body, appraising, measuring. She wished he'd keep his gaze on the road ahead – driving up here always made her nervous, with the road so close to the edge of the cliffs, nothing but a flimsy barrier between you and the rocks far below.

'Sorry,' Evan said, causing Kate to stare at him in astonishment. He was apologising? Well, that was a first. 'But,' he continued, 'don't you think you're giving your mum a bit of a hard time? I mean, she didn't exactly steal your son. She's just borrowed him for a while.'

Another sideways glance told her that Evan was joking again, and suddenly she felt tired of him, tired of the way he could never take anything seriously, not even something as serious as this.

'Sam isn't only my son,' she said.

'Well, quite,' Evan agreed. 'Which is why your darling mother contacted me in the first place.'

'And you still haven't told me why that was,' Kate reminded him. 'Despite just saying that you would.'

'It's obvious, isn't it? I've come for my son.'

Kate felt a chill creep up her spine. 'What do you mean, you've come for your son? If she won't give him to me she certainly won't give him to you.'

'What makes you think that?'

'Evan, stop playing with me. I don't deserve this. You abandoned Sam and me, you left us with nothing – no money, no food, nothing. You knew I was struggling, that I needed you, but you left anyway. And I haven't heard a thing from you until now. Don't I deserve to have at least one proper conversation where you tell it like it really is?'

'You could have had that on Saturday, Kate my darling. But your new boyfriend put paid to that.'

'He's not my boyfriend,' she said hotly. She was about to say more, but caught herself in time. It was obvious what he was doing; he'd always known how to play with her emotions.

'Evan, please stop trying to wind me up. Let's just discuss this like grown-ups, okay?'

'Sure, Kate. Whatever you say.'

He swung the car into a parking space, then turned to face her head on. 'But you really do look good, Kate. You're wasted on the country bumpkins around here.'

Kate sighed, already exhausted. Being with Evan was like sparring with a shadow. She said, 'What does my mother want you to do for her?'

'Straight to the point, same as always. Why do you think she wants me to do anything for her?' He laughed as Kate narrowed her eyes at him. 'Okay, fine. She wants me to help her, of course. Why else would she track me down and fly me here to this dump?'

He waved his arm to take in the car park at the top of the cliff and everything around it. Kate thought again how different they were: he really was a city boy, comfortable only with the throb of traffic and the dirty grey air and the clamour of thousands of people all rammed into one small space. She could see only beauty here, although it was a beauty she had long forgotten.

'And how, precisely, does she want you to help her?' Kate asked, her voice steady and patient.

For the first time, Evan looked uncomfortable. Kate knew it was her calm assurance that was throwing him, and she determined to keep it up, no matter how much he provoked her.

'Go on,' she said, smiling. 'Whatever it is, I won't blame you. After all, you're only doing what's best for

Sam, right?'

'Right,' Evan agreed, but now he didn't sound so sure. 'Well, she wants me to, like, testify or something. Tell the court what you used to do – what we used to do – back in Manchester.'

'I see.' It was only what Kate had expected, but she was still shocked at her mother's capacity for pure self-interest. 'And are you going to do that?'

Evan shrugged. 'If they swear me in, Kate, I'll have to tell the truth, the whole truth, and nothing but the –'

'It's not a bloody criminal court,' she snapped. 'You won't be interrogated by lawyers in white wigs.' But then she wondered if Evan was right – was that how it would be on the day? And if so, where would Evan's testimony leave her? Looking very bad, that was for sure. Coupled with the police report Elizabeth had shown her, she would look very bad indeed.

'I haven't said I'll do it,' Evan told her. He reached across and laid his hand lightly on her knee. 'I've got no desire to hurt you.'

'Shall we get that drink now?' Kate threw open the car door and made her escape. But once she was outside in the fresh air she couldn't face sitting indoors again. She didn't want to be confined with Evan, was already dreading the short journey home. She thought, not for the first time, that as soon as she had Sam back and had sorted herself out financially she would need to learn to drive and look out for a cheap car. She couldn't be dependent on taxis and buses and lifts forever. She wanted to be self-sufficient, to have to rely on no one.

She suggested a walk along the cliff, but Evan baulked at his; clearly he wasn't used to the fresh air or the bracing wind, and was already turning up the collar of his shirt against it. They returned to the car, and this time Evan did open her door first.

'Kate, can I ask you something?'

She paused, her hand resting lightly on the roof of the car. 'Sure. Go ahead.'

'Why do you want Sam back so badly? I mean, you could have it all now. Your mum looking after him for you, while you get your life back on track, live a little, all the while having the best of both worlds. Why are you so set on making it harder for yourself?'

Kate bit back a retort, realising that for once he was deadly serious. 'You really don't know, do you? You have no desire to be with your son, never have had.' She shook her head. It was unbelievable – or at least it would be, if this was anyone other than him. 'Let me ask you something, Evan. Have you seen Sam yet? Has she let you meet him?'

He shrugged. 'He was in bed when I went round. I'm sure I'll see him soon.'

'And that's it? You're not curious, you don't feel a pull, an attachment? Nothing at all?'

'I'm not like you, Kate. My life is more ... fluid.'

Well, that was one way of putting it. Kate regarded him for a moment, considering.

'You asked me a straight question, so I'll give you a straight answer. I want Sam back because he belongs with me. Because the world will always feel wrong until he's by my side again. He's mine, and I love him with all my heart. Every moment I'm away from him is like a knife in my heart. And the only freedom I want in my life is the freedom to be with my son. Does that answer your question?'

Evan stepped closer. She could smell his aftershave, the same type he'd always used, although for the life of her she couldn't remember what it was called. Some memories weren't worth clinging onto, after all.

'I admire that, Kate. I really do. And you know, just because your mother asked me to speak up for her, doesn't mean I have to. It would be just as easy for me say that you never smoked pot, that you were a model citizen. I'd do it,' he said, stepping closer still, 'if you asked me to.'

Kate tried to shift away from him, but she was trapped against the car. 'I don't want you to lie in court, Evan. Just tell the truth. I've done nothing I need to be ashamed of – plenty of people make mistakes when they're younger. They still go on to be good parents. I've got no desire to be painted as some kind of paragon. I'm just me. The fact that I'm Sam's mum will be enough.'

'Will it, though?' Evan murmured, his breath touching her face. 'Your mother is a very determined lady. I wouldn't bet against her, if I were you.'

'You're not me,' Kate countered. She fought the urge to push him away, not wanting to spark a fight – she knew how volatile Evan could be. Like her father. They were so similar. Addictive personalities, a penchant for losing themselves in intoxication, a tendency to fly off the handle when things didn't go their way. She forced a smile onto her face, keeping it light. 'I have nothing to give you, Evan. Whatever you choose to do, it's up to you. Just try not to make it any worse for Sam. That's all I ask.'

'I wouldn't say you have nothing to give.' Evan pushed himself against her, but then moved away so quickly she had no time to react. In a flash he had rounded the car and was sitting in the driver's seat, grinning up at her inanely. 'Get in, then. About time I got you home.'

Kate slipped into the car and strapped herself in. Her head was reeling; but wasn't this what it was always like being around Evan? Like being on a roller coaster in high winds, the earth falling away then lurching back at you, only to fall away again. He drove back along the coast road with his elbow leaning out of the open window, his hair blowing back from his clear, untroubled brow. It was only when they pulled up outside the house on Bow Hill that he brought Sam up again, and this time Kate was completely unprepared.

'You know,' he said, staying her hand as she began to undo her seat belt, 'the perfect solution would be for you and me to give it another go. Your mother needn't know anything about it – I could let her think I was on her side right until the day of the court hearing. And then we could be a proper family again. It would be just like old times, Kate. You and me – we were good together, you can't deny it.'

'And what about the money?' Kate said. 'I haven't got any, Evan. I know she's paying you to do this for her. I'm not stupid. I know you too well.'

He shrugged. 'Like I said, she doesn't need to know. We'll take her money and use it to set ourselves up somewhere. I've got a mate in Scotland, he's got this business idea – a sure-fire winner. It's different this time. Totally above board. And you'll be far away from her, you and Sam. You'd never have to face her again.'

Kate looked out of the window. She saw the net curtain at Marie's window shift a little. What would Marie say about an offer like this? Kate looked back at Evan. 'You don't want me and Sam, not really. If you did, you'd have come back for me before.'

'I was in a mess, Kate. I got in … I was in a bit of trouble before you and I broke up. To be honest, it was why I took off. I didn't want you and Sam to be involved. There was this bloke, he was bad news – I mean, really bad news. I knew if he found out I had a missus and a kid he'd have leverage over me. So I did the decent thing and legged it.' He gazed at her, his eyes wide and clear. 'I did it because I love you.'

Kate laughed. 'Oh, you are very good. Did she help you make up that story? It's very plausible, I'll give you that. But a total load of bollocks.'

'No, Kate. It's the truth. I always intended coming back for you. It just took a little longer than I planned.'

'Well, why didn't you tell me? You just took off after a row, Evan. I do remember that much – the bang on the head didn't wipe out my memory completely.'

'It didn't?' He was silent for a moment. She thought she saw real concern in his eyes, but she could have been wrong. Lord knows, she'd been wrong before. 'So, do the police have any idea who did this to you?' he said, clenching his fists on the steering wheel. 'I'd like to get my hands on them, the low-life bastards.'

'They're totally in the dark. You know about the drugs, right? That were found in the flat?'

Evan nodded. 'Your mother mentioned that.'

'I bet she did. What she probably didn't tell you is that I have no idea how they got there. I'd left that behind me. You know I had.'

He said nothing, but for a moment Kate saw a kind of sadness pass across his face. She felt for him, if only a little. Evan was a mess, despite the sharp designer shirt and the swept back hair and the luminous sports car. She wondered whether his offer was genuine. Although there would have to be something in it for him, something she hadn't figured out yet. With Evan, there was always a price to pay.

'Say I agreed, Evan. Say I came with you to Scotland and started again, you, me and Sam. How do I know I could trust you? You've let me down before. What's to stop you doing it again?'

He held out his hands, palms up. 'But you can't lose, Kate. You get your son back and you're free of your mother. Plus you get one up on her, which – after the way she's treated you – seems like reason enough for me.' He dropped his voice and inched closer. 'It was never really over for us, Kate. Not really. You've always been the one and only for me. And if you're honest with yourself, you know I'm the only one for you.' He leaned towards her, his body clearing the console that separated the seats, and before Kate knew what was happening he was kissing her, one hand behind her head, the other cradling her cheek. His kiss was gentle but insistent, and Kate could feel her body responding as though out of habit; that touch, that scent, the flick of his tongue inside her mouth. The curve of his shoulders as her own hands reached out to hold him, momentarily forgetting everything, only feeling, remembering.

But then the spell was broken. She heard a door slam in the street, and she pushed herself out of Evan's embrace in time to see Patrick walking away from them, heading down the hill towards the beach. He was wearing his khaki shorts and a tight white T-shirt, and Kate felt her stomach lurch all over again. Patrick didn't look back, but he didn't have to. Kate could tell by the way he held his head, by the tightness of his gait, that he had seen them.

She turned to Evan and shook her head. 'You shouldn't have done that.'

'I know,' he said, but he was grinning broadly, clearly not sorry at all.

'You've only been back a couple of days. You can't just throw all this at me, and then dive on me and expect us to take up where we left off.'

'I know,' he said again.

She grabbed her bag and told him goodbye, scrabbling to get out of the car before he could grab her again. Patrick was halfway down the street now, but still he hadn't turned around. She wished he'd come back so she could explain. She thought about running after him, but then she realised how ridiculous that would look.

'Will you think about it?' Evan called, still leaning across the passenger seat. Kate rolled her eyes, but she nodded.

'I might. But don't pressure me. And stay away from my mother.'

He gave her a salute, then fired up the engine and pulled out from the kerb.

'Just don't make anything worse than it already is,' Kate called, but Evan was already speeding away.

No matter. Kate already knew what she was going to do. This was her son's life they were talking about, not some kind of game.

And her mother would not be pulling anyone's strings, least of all Evan's.

Chapter 17

'What are you doing here?' Barbara said. She looked around outside for her daughter but the social worker was alone.

'It's just a flying visit, Mrs Steiner, I hope you don't mind.'

'What is it concerning?'

But the social worker was already stepping inside and unbuttoning her coat, smiling at Barbara as though they were old friends. 'Getting cold so quickly, don't you think?' she said, making little shivery gestures with her shoulders.

Barbara didn't respond. She braced herself against the hall table, her hands behind her back. 'Is this to do with Samuel?'

Elizabeth nodded. 'Mrs Steiner, I'm here at your daughter's request, to talk to you about some very troubling accusations made by Samuel's father, Evan. Apparently, you have offered to pay him to speak up for you during the court hearing. Now–'

'He's going to tell the truth, that's all,' Barbara cried. 'The judge has a right to know what kind of a person she is.'

'Did you offer to pay money to this man to speak for you in court?'

'No.' Barbara turned and brushed invisible dust off the polished table, then straightened a studio photo of Samuel posed on red satin. 'No, I did not.'

'Well, I'm pleased to hear that, because it would be a criminal offence to try to manipulate a court hearing and I would have to bring it to the attention of the police.'

Barbara laughed. 'She sent you here to intimidate me, did she? Well, I'm just an old lady who loves her grandson. I've got nothing and no one on my side. She's got all the cards stacked in her favour, don't you see? So I asked Samuel's dad to speak for me – why does that make me a bad person?'

Elizabeth shook back her hair, then produced a pair of woollen gloves from her pocket and began to pull them on. 'Mrs Steiner, you and Kate should talk. I mean, really talk. There's still time for you to make a joint arrangement over this. It sounds to me like it is starting to get out of hand.'

'She's no saint,' Barbara said hotly. 'She's been round here, throwing around all sorts of accusations. Dragging up the past. You want to talk to her about her behaviour. She has issues, you know. She's not ready to be a mother.'

'Samuel will be the one to suffer in the long run if you and your daughter are at each other's throats. And Kate said ...' Elizabeth tailed off, shaking her head.

'What? What did she say?'

The social worker sighed heavily. 'Just that Evan is a liability. He's already offered to share your money with Kate and string you along until the last minute. She wanted you to know that she's not playing games. She wants you to know you can trust her but you can't trust him.'

'Rubbish,' Barbara said automatically, but her brain was working hard, trying to process what this woman was telling her. Evan was a liability alright. But right now, he was all she had on her side.

Barbara closed the door and leaned her forehead against it briefly. She turned around and jumped, her hand flying up to her mouth.

David was standing directly behind her.

'And what,' he said, his face as grey as stone, 'was all that about?'

***

'You can take that look off your face right away, David. You're no saint so don't bloody well judge me.'

Her husband blinked and looked away. But then he swung back to face her, his expression hard. 'No, I'm no saint. You're right. And I'm only just beginning to realise the extent of my mistakes and the damage I've done. I was hoping to be able to put things right, but you seem to have this ... agenda. I don't know you anymore, Barb.'

'What does that mean – put things right? Are you going to steal Samuel away from under my nose and take him to Kate? Because I'm telling you now, David, if you even try such a thing I'll –'

'Don't be stupid, woman. You're becoming hysterical. I care about that boy. Whatever happens has to be done properly.' He regarded her through narrowed eyes. 'No one around here seems to be sinking to that kind of level except you. What the hell were you playing at, getting that man involved? You said he was a criminal, a drug dealer. Have you lost your mind?'

Barbara sat down suddenly on the narrow wooden bench behind her. Coats hung off hooks, draping over her shoulders; by her feet was a basket of outdoor shoes and three pairs of slippers for guests to wear in the house. It had been years since any guests had come to stay in the house.

'Don't worry about Evan,' she said. 'I can handle him.'

'Can you? I doubt it. But what about Kate? How did

you think she would feel, seeing him again? Why must you keep punishing her like this?'

'Me? I'm punishing her? Oh, that's rich coming from the man who used to terrify her so much she'd wet the bed twice a week.'

As soon as the words were out of her mouth, Barbara wished she could take them back. She held her breath, her eyes wide and startled.

Her husband crumpled before her eyes, slumping forward towards the hall stand, holding onto the coat hooks for support. Barbara jumped up and put her arms around his back. She couldn't afford for him to lose it now. A crisis of conscience would be fatal. Somehow she had to get him back on side with her.

'It wasn't your fault,' she told him, stroking his rounded back with her thin hand. 'She always was a difficult child, always bleating and moaning, looking at us with those judging eyes – it must have driven you crazy. And I didn't help, did I? The things I did to wind you up, not really understanding it from your point of view ... It must have been so hard.'

She paused, thinking of where to go next, but before she could say another word David twisted himself out from between her arms and pushed her bodily away from him.

'Get off me. You disgust me, Barbara. You disgust me through to my bones. I was a terrible father to Kate, a drunk and a tyrant, and I've denied it to myself for far too long. It's time to try and make amends. I can only hope it's not too late for me ... But you, yes, you're right. You are as bad as me. You will stop at nothing to get what you want, even blaming your own daughter, your own child, for what I did to her – what we did to her.'

He flung her hands from him as she tried to grab at his wrists. Barbara looked up at her husband's face and what she saw there was more terrifying than the anger she'd faced down so many times before.

'You're on your own in this, woman,' he told her through gritted teeth. 'I'm not going to fall in with your sick plans anymore. And anything I can do to help Kate, I will. It may not be too late for me and her. If I can make her see how sorry I am, if I can just make her see … But it's too late for you. She'll get her son back, don't you doubt it for one minute, and maybe one day she'll forgive me. But you'll have nothing and no one. And it will serve you bloody well right.'

Chapter 18

On Friday, Kate got up and washed quickly in the en suite sink, pulling her thin dressing gown more tightly around her as the early morning chill made goose bumps rise on her arms. Soon it would be October; already the heat was draining from the days, the darkening evenings bringing with them an autumnal feel. She cleaned her teeth and listened to Patrick moving around above her. They'd hardly spoken since the previous weekend. Kate had the feeling he was keeping out of her way. She sighed and spat out a mouthful of froth. She didn't blame him. First her ex turns up, then her crazy mother chases them down the driveway, and then he sees her kissing Evan in the street. It was unlikely Patrick would want to get involved in anything so messy. It was a shame, though. Her body, asleep for far too long, had woken up in Patrick's arms, and now it seemed unwilling to forget his burning touch.

As soon as she was dressed, Kate sat down at her sewing machine, forgoing her usual morning walk in light of more pressing matters. A group of Marie's friends had heard about Kate's dressmaking skills, no doubt from Marie's own lips, and had brought over a bag full of clothes needing alterations: a pair of trousers that sagged at the waist, a designer skirt needing shortening, three dresses to let out around the waistline, and a bolero jacket with a piping trim that needed repairing.

'This is amazing,' Kate had gushed, but Marie wouldn't take any credit.

'You're getting work from your own advert, too,' she pointed out. 'And make sure you charge this lot good money. They can afford it.'

Kate grabbed the first item off the top of the bag and set to work with her unpicker. She'd have to redo the waistband completely, she decided, in order to do a professional job. Designer clothes were a little outside her comfort zone, confined as she'd been up till now to children's clothing and vintage dress patterns, but she worked methodically and soon began to enjoy herself. Just after ten, Marie came up with coffee, nodding her approval when she saw how much Kate had done.

'They'll have to come in for a proper fitting,' Kate said, holding up the trousers. They looked rather forlorn with their interfacing exposed and the back seam half unpicked.

'Of course,' Marie agreed. 'Those belong to Laura – did I tell you she lost ten pounds this summer?'

Kate grinned. Only about a hundred times. Losing weight was Marie's latest obsession, along with worry about her wrinkles and being paranoid about looking old. Marie was pacing now, picking up random objects and putting them down again. She sighed heavily, then flopped down onto Kate's neatly made bed.

'I don't know, Kate. I'm starting to wonder if it's all worth it.'

'What do you mean?' Kate grabbed her coffee and pulled her chair closer to her friend.

'Oh, it's nothing really. Just silly old me.'

'Marie.' Kate regarded her friend over the rim of the mug. 'What's wrong?'

'It's Big Tony,' Marie said, sighing again, her shoulders slumping. 'I think he might be losing interest in me again. He hasn't called in a few days. He's probably seeing someone else.'

'No! Surely not?' Kate was genuinely shocked. From what she'd heard, Big Tony was a reformed character. 'He wouldn't do that to you.'

'Wouldn't he?' Marie pulled a rueful face. 'He's done it before. Many times.'

Kate's thoughts returned to Evan, who had been texting her constantly these past few days, pressuring her to make a decision. She'd kept his offer to herself, unwilling to listen to Marie's inevitable 'I told you so.'

'Come on,' Kate said, pulling her chair a little closer. 'Tell me what's happened.'

'Nothing.' Marie shook her head. 'Forget I said it. Look, what's that you've got out over there? They look like photos.'

Marie crossed the room and collected up the photographs Kate had scattered across the floor the previous night.

'They're from the box that was in storage,' Kate explained. 'I keep going through them, trying to piece it all together.'

'You mean the attack?'

Kate nodded. 'There must be something I can do to try and remember. I just keep thinking the answer is there in my memory somewhere. If only I could access it. I want so badly to be able to put it to bed, you know? To understand what happened leading up to the attack, and to know for sure who, if anyone, planted those drugs.'

'If anyone?' Marie picked up on Kate's tone at once. 'Are you saying what I think you're saying?'

Kate lifted her shoulders briefly. 'I don't know. That's the problem – I don't know. Maybe it was me. Maybe I had started smoking again, just as a way to cope. I was lonely, I know I was struggling. And you know what they say – old habits die hard.'

'No. I won't have it, Kate. You were – you are – a good mother, and you wouldn't have done that with Sam in the house. No matter how lonely or depressed you were.'

'Maybe I was in pain? It works for pain. I had a friend up north who used to take it for her migraines. She'd bake it into chocolate brownies.'

'Brownies?' Marie laughed. 'Well, I've heard everything now. Do you have the recipe?'

Kate laughed too, but then her expression grew sombre. 'I'm certain it wasn't me, but if it wasn't then how did those packages get inside the toilet? If I could just clear that up, prove I am one hundred percent blameless, I'd feel so much better about this court hearing. Especially with Evan on the scene again. He's such a wild card, Marie. You never know what's going to happen with him around.'

'Maybe it was him,' Marie suggested. 'Maybe you were getting back together and he left them there.'

Kate shook her head. 'No, he was already in Scotland by then. And we weren't getting back together, I'd definitely remember that. Besides, I asked him about it already. He's just as much in the dark as I am.' She sighed and took the photos out of Marie's hands. 'Memory is a funny thing. I remember almost everything now, but the day of the break-in is still a total blank.'

'Do you still get the nightmares?'

Kate nodded grimly. 'And I still believe that if I could only bring myself to turn around in my dream, I'd see who it was. I think that's what happened, in real life I mean. That I turned around and caught the intruder.'

'And that's why he knocked you out,' Marie added.

They sat together in silence for a while, staring at the floor, each locked in their private world of memory and regret. Kate's phone began to vibrate; she glanced at it but didn't recognise the number.

'I'll wait and see if they leave a message,' she said. But even as she spoke the house phone began to ring in the hallway, and Marie heaved herself up to answer it. Kate waited, listening to the ticking of her watch, the creaking of the old house as it settled into itself. Sometimes, she thought, you just have a sense for bad news. When it turns out you were wrong you forget all about it, but if you're right, you remember those moments before you heard the news for the rest of your life.

'Kate.'

Marie stood in her doorway, her face drained of colour. For a second Kate reflected that Marie really shouldn't die her hair that flat black shade; it did absolutely nothing for her.

'It's for you,' Marie said, handing her the cordless phone as though it was made of china. Kate tucked the phone to her ear, but reeled back as soon as she heard her mother's voice screeching down the line.

'Kate? Kate, are you there? Is that you? Your father is in hospital, fighting for his life. Are you happy now? This is all your doing, the stress, the worry, all your fault. You've killed him, Kate. And I will never, ever forgive you.'

***

At the hospital, Kate prowled the waiting room, throwing occasional glances at her mother, who sat apart from them staring into space. The woman hadn't spoken since they'd arrived, but the accusations she'd thrown at Kate still rang in her ears.

'Looks like she's finally sobered up,' Kate whispered to Marie, coming to rest next to her on one of the green upholstered chairs. Patrick sat on Marie's other side. He'd brought them here, answering Marie's frantic phone call with a calm voice and an instruction to sit tight and wait for him.

But now he looked out of place, too vivid and outdoorsy to be cooped up in this bland, scrubbed-down space, and Kate wished he'd just dropped them at the front entrance and gone back to work as she'd asked. She almost wished he'd taken Marie with him. Who were these people, really? She only knew them by virtue of fate; if Elizabeth had found her a different place to lodge she'd never have met them at all. And yet, here they were, closer to her than her own family. Far closer than that distant woman over there.

She looked up at a notice board filled with brightly coloured posters for various support groups. One of them offered bereavement counselling. Kate turned away from it, offended. Marie twisted her hands together and chewed on her lip; she'd already bitten off all her bright red lipstick, and her hair looked like she'd been dragged through a hedge. Anyone would think it was Marie's father in there, not Kate's. But she knew it was Barbara's presence that had sent Marie into a frenzy. Her friend was conflicted, wanting to offer comfort to the wife of a desperately sick man, while at the same time feeling a deep antipathy for the woman who was causing Kate so much pain.

Welcome to my world, Kate thought, getting up to resume her pacing.

She tried to picture her father on the operating table while surgeons battled to restart his heart and put him back together again. Like Humpty Dumpty. But her dad hadn't just fallen off a wall, had he? He'd been well and truly pushed.

'Oh, God.' She dropped her head into her hands. An arm snaked around her shoulder, and she looked up to see Patrick by her side. He pulled her close, then released her just as quickly.

'It will be okay,' he said. 'He's in the best possible

place.'

Kate stared at him, her eyes pleading. 'I did this, didn't I? If I hadn't told Elizabeth about Evan, if she hadn't gone over there ...' She put her face against his chest, suddenly glad he was here after all. 'I hate him,' she said quietly. 'But I don't want him to die. Does that make any sense at all?'

'It makes perfect sense.' Patrick spoke in a low voice for her ears only. She listened, focusing on the weave of his shirt, the smell of his body. 'Kate, the fact that this happened during an argument is irrelevant. They might not even have been arguing about you. And it sounds to me like neither of your parents are strangers to arguing. You mustn't blame yourself. Yes, your dad found out about your mother's behaviour, but it would have come out soon enough. Besides, I don't think his heart attack had anything to do with that.'

She blinked through her tears. 'You don't?'

'You say he was ill last year? Well, maybe there was an underlying condition. And he'd been ... Well, you said he was a drinker. He probably wasn't in the best of health to start with.'

Patrick was right. Kate knew it, but she couldn't shake the feeling of dread in her stomach. Her mother said that they were arguing about her, that he was angry about her. She said Kate had broken his heart.

But what about her heart?

'If he dies, what will I do? There is so much I need to say, things I need to know.'

Patrick led her back to Marie. Kate glanced at her mother surreptitiously, hoping to see some emotion on her face, a sign that what was happening was actually getting through. The woman looked as though she was doing nothing more onerous than waiting for an appointment at the dentist.

'I've been thinking,' Marie said, still twisting her

hands in her lap. 'I have a theory about your dad. It could be complete rubbish, but it might explain a few things.'

Kate smiled weakly. She was glad now that Marie was here too. Her down-to-earth solidarity was just what she needed right now. 'Go on,' she said.

'Well,' Marie continued, 'do you think your father might have felt guilty? You said you had a horrible childhood, that he'd been a heavy drinker, that you were scared of him. Do you think that he wanted to make amends for that?'

Kate shook her head. 'He never even acknowledged that he had done anything wrong. The day I left home I confronted him with it. Of course, by that time it hadn't happened for a few years because I was that bit older and I guess he couldn't intimidate me the way he had before. But I brought it all out into the open that day. He had a chance to say sorry. I might even have forgiven him then. I wanted to have it settled.' Kate felt a pain in her chest as she remembered that conversation, the last she would have with her father for years. 'He denied everything. Told me I was a fantasist, an attention seeker. My mother – she sat next to him, looked me in the eyes and agreed.'

Patrick's face hardened. Kate wondered what he was thinking.

'I can't imagine how horrible it was for you,' Marie said with a shudder. 'But you did say that your mother told you the other day that he was on your side now, that he wanted you to have Sam back?'

'Yes, but that was just because he couldn't be bothered looking after him anymore,' Kate countered.

'Oh, come on. That can't be right. They took Sam on in the first place, didn't they? Your dad was retired, your mum's not getting any younger. It can't have been easy, taking on a baby. With your mum, maybe she just needed to feel needed. But your dad? If he was still the tyrant you believed him to be, he would have said no way.' Marie shrugged. 'But he didn't, did he? He chose to look after Sam and give him a comfortable home, and as far as we know he's treated him well. Perhaps he was trying to make up for all the things he'd done to you.'

'Sam certainly seems to love his granddad,' Kate admitted. She thought about how upset her son would be when he heard his granddad was poorly. Barbara had left Sam with his friend's family on the way to the hospital, so at least he would be protected from all this until they knew more. Kate looked down the corridor in the direction they'd taken her father and wondered again how he was holding up.

She looked at Marie with a new-found respect. 'I honestly hadn't thought about it that way,' she said, shrugging. 'Although you're just imagining how you might feel and putting those feelings onto him. Which is because you're a nice person. I'm not so sure what kind of a person he is these days.'

'Well, as soon as he's out of surgery you can ask him, can't you?' Marie said briskly, patting Kate's hand.

Kate nodded. All she wanted to do now was see her son and give him a hug. She couldn't believe how much she missed him. The hearing was only two weeks away. And maybe, just maybe, this would be a turning point for all of them. Maybe after this they could put the past behind them once and for all and move forward. For Sam's sake. For all their sakes.

A doctor came into view, loping along the corridor in his white coat. He made a beeline for Kate's mother, leaning low to talk to her. Both of them ignored Kate. She felt her friends grow tense beside her but she said nothing. When her mother got up and followed the doctor back down the corridor, Kate swallowed over a lump in her throat. He must have come round after the surgery and asked for Barbara. She wondered if he'd ask to see her soon. Half of her wanted to see him very much; the other half wanted to run a mile.

But more than anything she hoped that Marie's hunch was right, and that her father was ready to admit the truth and say he was sorry. Sorry couldn't give her back all those years, the sleepless nights, the fear and the loneliness. But it could pave the way to a better future, one without bitterness and recriminations. In a couple of months it would be Christmas. She tried to picture them all sitting around her mother's enormous dining table, eating turkey, pulling crackers, wearing silly hats. It was possible, she told herself. Unlikely, but possible.

Anything was possible, after all.

Patrick and Marie had gone off in search of the cafeteria when Barbara reappeared. She walked along the corridor as if in a trance, pausing at the entrance to the waiting area, looking around at the faces blankly. There were three other families there now, so Kate waved to get her attention, then dropped her arm to her side, feeling stupid. Her mother's face was dark and clouded. She sat next to Kate and looked at her hands.

'Have you been in with Dad?' Kate asked. 'How is he?'

Barbara laughed. She turned to face her daughter, and Kate drew back when she saw the look in her eyes.

'What are you doing here, Kate?'

'What? I don't – what do you mean?'

'Why are you here? You made no secret of the fact that you hated your father, so what is all this about?' Barbara leaned forward, her face a ghastly white. 'Is it guilt?' she asked.

'I don't have anything to feel guilty about.' Kate spoke hotly. Where were Patrick and Marie? She didn't feel able to deal with her mother's moods anymore. 'Look, I'm not discussing this with you now. Not here.

I'll go in and see Dad, and then I'll going home. In a few days, when everything's calmed down a bit, maybe we can talk again.' She took a deep breath, let it out as slowly as she could. 'So. Would you mind telling me which room he's in so I can go to him.'

Kate could feel her mother's eyes on her face. She didn't want to look at her, didn't want to see her thoughts written so clearly there. Fine, Kate thought, blame me if you like. If it makes you feel better. But if you hadn't gone after Evan, if you hadn't taken things so far ...

'You can't go and see him.'

'What do you mean, I can't? You can't stop me. If I want to talk to him I will. He's my father.'

'Not anymore he's not,' her mother said with a grim smile.

Kate shook her head. What new game was this?

Barbara's voice was no more than a rumble. 'How many times have you wished he was dead. Go on, be honest. You might as well now, you've nothing to lose. You hated him enough to want him dead, and now your wish has come true. You've finally managed to get your revenge, Kate. Your father is dead.'

It couldn't be true. Her mother was lying. This was her latest trick. But then, even as Kate tried to form the words that would expose the wicked lie, she saw Patrick talking to a doctor. It was the same doctor, improbably young, impossibly tired. She saw Marie turn and look at her, her expression one of almost comical concern. Kate pushed her chair away, scraping it across the floor, and began to run. Away from her mother, and from Patrick and Marie and their pitying eyes; away from the hospital where her father lay still now, unable to ever tell her himself that he was sorry for the things he'd done.

She found herself outside the main building, her mind numb. She slipped between two wheelie bins and sank to the floor, hidden from view. My father is dead, she said to herself, and then she said it out loud. 'My father is dead.' It didn't make it any more real. One minute he'd been there, his face red with anger, his breath a whiskey-fuelled fire, and the next he was gone. She tried to focus on how it made her feel, whether all those feelings of hatred and anger she'd held on to for so many years would go now, just dissolve into nothingness. After a while she realised they hadn't, and they probably never would. They had merely receded and been replaced by a dull sadness. Regret was a bitter pill indeed.

She started to run again. Gone was the stiffness in her legs; she was stronger now, stronger than she'd ever been before. The lights of the hospital buildings faded behind her as she ran on into the welcoming darkness. She had no idea where she was. She had no idea what to do next. She knew one thing and one thing only, and this she repeated to herself like a mantra as her feet pounded the pavement and the buildings sped by in a blur. She still had Sam. Soon Sam would be home. Hold on just a little bit longer. Your son is coming home.

Chapter 19

Eventually, Kate found her way back to Bow Hill, surprised to see all the lights on in the house, even those in her own room. It was after dark now; she looked at her watch and saw it was almost eight. Marie dived out of her door as soon as Kate's key turned in the lock.

'Oh, Kate, where have you been?'

'I just needed to be on my own.' Kate didn't want to meet her friend's eye, couldn't bear to see the look of concern there. 'I still do, I'm afraid. Please don't be offended.'

'Never mind about all that,' Marie said, bustling Kate towards the stairs. 'You need to sort your head out and put on a big smile.'

'I don't think this is the time for keeping up appearances.' She was about to say more, but Marie held up her hand and cut her off.

'Sam's upstairs,' she said. Kate's mouth dropped open.

'He's where?'

'Upstairs. With Elizabeth.' Marie was already on her way up, talking over her shoulder; Kate followed closely behind, her feet hardly touching the treads.

'How long's he been here? And why? I mean, what did Elizabeth say?'

'Ask her yourself,' Marie said with a soft smile. She stepped out of the way to allow Kate past. Kate felt a touch on her back, a pat of reassurance, and then she opened the door to her room and stepped inside.

Sam was sitting on her bed wearing spotty pyjamas and cuddling a teddy. He was watching something on a tablet device propped against Kate's bedside lamp, one thumb jammed into his mouth. When Kate walked in his eyes flicked to her briefly, but he didn't register her beyond that one small gesture. Elizabeth, who was sitting at the sewing table gazing at her phone, looked up and smiled, then she stood and gestured to Kate to follow her through to the other room.

'What's going on?' Kate asked, her voice low but insistent.

'I'm sorry about your father,' Elizabeth said. 'It must have been a horrible shock. Did you know he had heart problems?'

Kate shook her head. She would process her feelings about her father soon enough, but right now her thoughts were firmly on the little boy sitting all alone in her bedroom.

'What's Sam doing here?' she asked again. Was it too much to hope that this was it now, that Sam was going to be with her for good?

Perhaps her mother had had a change of heart, realising she couldn't cope alone ...

'It's just for tonight, Kate,' Elizabeth said, as though she could see Kate's hope flashing across her eyes like the scenes on a TV screen. 'I thought it would be best for him to stay somewhere else – your mother will be at the hospital for a while yet, and I doubt she'll be in any fit state to look after a toddler when she does get home. As soon as I heard I went to his friend's house and collected him.' Elizabeth looked around the room, which was empty apart from an old low wardrobe and an upholstered armchair that Kate had hauled home from the thrift shop.

'This is Sam's room,' Kate explained, 'except I haven't

got much furniture for it. But it's fine, he can sleep with me tonight. I mean, he can have my bed and I'll sleep on the floor,' she added, seeing the dubious look on the social worker's face. 'Honestly, Elizabeth, it'll be fine. You did the right thing bringing him here. And –' she swallowed, peering through the open door at her son. Her son! 'And thank you,' she finished. 'Thank you so much.'

'It's only for one night,' Elizabeth repeated. 'If your mother insists on having him back tomorrow we'd better go along with that for now. This close to the court hearing, it's not a good idea to cause friction. We want it to look like you are totally reasonable and amenable.'

'Which I am,' Kate reminded her, walking back into her bedroom. 'Hey, Sam. How are you doing? What do you think of your ... of my pad?'

He gazed up at her blankly. His eyes were red-rimmed and his mouth had a blurry look to it.

'He's just tired,' Elizabeth said, gathering up her things. 'He's a sensitive kid, Kate. I think he's figured out there's something going on.' She shut down the tablet, invoking a cry of protest from Sam.

'Watch telly!' he demanded, thrashing his legs on top of the duvet. Elizabeth glanced around the room, then raised her eyes at Kate.

'I haven't got around to buying one yet,' Kate said, feeling her face pink up. All of a sudden she felt completely inadequate – all this time she'd been sitting around feeling sorry for herself, day dreaming about how wonderful it would be to have Sam home with her, making clothes for him, making plans, but she hadn't done one single practical thing like paint his room or buy a bloody TV.

'Sure,' Elizabeth said, shrugging. 'It doesn't matter, Kate. He needs love and attention, not to be stuck in front of a screen all day.' She looked at the small screen in her hand and gave a rueful smile, followed by another small shrug of her shoulders. She said, 'I'll be back in the morning to give Sam a ride back to his nana's, okay?'

'Not too early,' Kate called after her. 'Leave it till lunchtime if you like.'

She shut the door and turned around, her heart beating a fast dance in her chest. Sam was here. Whatever else had happened today, whatever was going on in the rest of the world right now, this was all that mattered.

'Have you eaten?' she asked him. He stared back at her, his expression wary. 'Are you hungry?' she said, trying again. 'I have some yummy crisps here, or you could have a cookie if you prefer?'

Thank goodness for her penchant for junk food. Sam nodded and pointed to the packet of cookies, then he nodded again when Kate offered him a glass of milk. She sat at the end of the bed and watched him eat. He kept his eyes averted, throwing quick glances her way every few minutes. What must he be thinking, she wondered? She wished she'd asked Elizabeth a few more questions about where Sam had been, about what the social worker had told him on the way over here.

Sam finished his snack, then swung his legs off the bed and stood, swaying a little, in the middle of the floor. 'Where's Nana?' he asked, gazing up at Kate. She crouched down so her face was level with his, longing to hold him, but holding back just a little longer, some instinct telling her not to crowd him, not to make him feel overwhelmed.

'Nana's at the hospital, Sam. With Pops. You'll see her tomorrow, okay? Tonight you're having a sleepover with me.'

He considered this for a while, then nodded. But his eyes kept roaming the room. And then Kate noticed that he had one hand pressed against the front of his pyjama bottoms.

'Do you need the bathroom?' she said.

Sam nodded.

'Oh, Sam,' Kate said, smiling. 'I'm so sorry. Come on, let's get you sorted out.'

She led him into the tiny en suite, but once inside she hesitated.

'Sam, I don't know if you ... Do you use a potty yet, or ...?' Her face burned with the shame of it. She was his mother. She didn't even know this basic fact about her own son.

'I got big boy pants,' he told her proudly, dropping his trousers to show her. He was wearing a pull-up nappy, and Kate was relieved to find a stack of spares in his overnight bag, along with a change of clothes, another teddy, a story book and a toothbrush. Elizabeth had thought of everything. She made him laugh while she changed him and brushed his teeth, pulling faces in the mirror and telling him how she'd hated having her teeth brushed too when she was a child.

'When you were a little boy?' Sam said, and Kate just grinned and kissed the top of his head.

Back in her bedroom, she surveyed the space, trying to work out how best to set up the sleeping arrangements. She was dragging the duvet off the bed when she heard a tentative knock at the door.

'Sorry to bother you,' Marie said, peering around the door, her eyes as wide as saucers. 'Just that we have a couple of things we thought you might need.'

'We?' Kate frowned, but Marie only tapped the side of her nose and then disappeared again. Kate could hear whispering outside on the landing. She sat on the bed with Sam pressed to her side, his eyes like moons in his bewildered face. And then Patrick walked in, throwing Sam a wide smile and carrying ... a cot! A beautiful white-painted cot with high sides and a snug-looking mattress.

'Oh, my!' Kate exclaimed. 'It's perfect.'

'That's not all,' Patrick said. He disappeared again, then came back into the room almost completely hidden behind an enormous box. Kate jumped up from the bed with a delighted cry.

'Sam, it's a TV!'

'He went out to the retail park as soon as Elizabeth arrived,' Marie said, coming in behind Patrick with a pile of fresh bedding in her arms. 'There's a DVD player there too, and some films for Sam to watch. I've had the mattress for the cot airing on the radiator downstairs for a bit – it might smell musty after being in the attic for a while but it's absolutely fine, really, and I've got some sheets here, but if he'd rather have a sleeping bag, or if that's too big then I can –'

'Marie.' Kate laid a hand on her arm. 'It's perfect. I honestly don't know how to thank you. And I'll pay you for the TV,' she said to Patrick.

'In buttons, probably,' he said with a wink. He set the TV up on one of Kate's spare chairs, then plugged in the DVD player, fiddling with the wires at the back until the screen came on in a burst of colour.

'Come on, now,' Marie told him, tugging at his sleeve. 'Let's leave them to it.'

'Thank you,' Kate said again, joy and gratitude swelling in her throat. Sam waved with one chubby hand, bouncing on the bed in excitement.

'Telly,' he said, his eyes gleaming.

Kate closed the door and turned to smile at her son. She looked at her watch, then pursed her lips. 'Well,' she said, 'okay. But only for a little while. And then it'll be time for you to go to bed.'

***

Sam fell asleep leaning against her halfway through a Winnie the Pooh movie; she carried him carefully to his cot and laid him inside it, covering him with a blanket and laying his beloved teddy by his side. And then she watched him. She sat on the floor and gazed through the bars, her eyes growing blurry with tears. Was there anything so heartrendingly vulnerable as a sleeping child? It was this, Kate realised, that she was missing out on. These moments of everyday joy that parents take for granted: the sight of your child asleep in the back of the car, their heads lolling, their faces perfect in repose; the sounds of laughter as they race around the house with friends, lost in an imaginary world you will never be part of, wouldn't want to be part of, but can smile and marvel at none the less. Running to you with a cut knee; asking for help opening a packet of crisps; a random hug offered in love, asking nothing in return.

If Kate didn't get Sam back she would miss out on all of this, no matter how many times she was allowed to visit him. And yet, if she was successful, her mother would be the one to miss out. For the first time, Kate truly understood what that meant.

She watched Sam sleep, and occasionally her own head drooped as sleep crept up on her stealthily. It couldn't keep her under its spell for long – she was determined not to miss a second of having her son at home, under her own roof. Sitting on the floor in the room that was to be his room, Kate made plans. Her determination grew. And she knew that no matter what, she would have him back.

If she couldn't have Sam, she would rather die.

Chapter 20

Elizabeth arrived at nine o'clock. Kate heard her talking to Marie, who was no doubt stalling her as best she could, trying to buy Kate a little more time.

'Sam,' she said, crouching by his side as he ate his toast and watched children's TV, his eyes clear and bright after a good night's sleep. 'Sam, in a minute or two you'll be going back to Nana's house.'

He glanced at her, mid-bite. 'Stay here?' he said. 'Stay with Mummy?'

She smiled and blinked back sudden tears. 'I wish you could, sweetheart. But you'll come back soon, right? Come and stay again?'

He nodded, then rammed the rest of the toast into his mouth. Come back soon and stay forever, Kate didn't add. But she thought it, and she hoped her thoughts would transmit themselves to Sam somehow.

'Are we all ready?' Elizabeth stuck her head round the door and raised her eyebrows at Kate. 'Did you have a good night?'

Kate only nodded. She couldn't imagine how words could explain the night she'd had, or how Elizabeth could even ask such a question.

'Give her my .... my best wishes,' Kate told Elizabeth once Sam was strapped into the car. 'Tell her I'm here whenever she's ready to talk.'

Elizabeth nodded once, then started up the engine and drove away.

Marie appeared by Kate's side. Together they watched the car until it disappeared at the bottom of Bow Hill. 'How are you bearing up?' she said.

'I'm fine,' Kate told her. 'Considering.'

'All set for tomorrow? Painting Sam's room, remember?' Marie reminded her gently. 'If you still feel up to it, that is. I know it's probably the last thing you feel like now.'

Kate shook her head. 'No, it'll be good to be doing something. Something practical. And it's so lovely of you to offer to help. And Patrick too. I don't deserve to have friends like you, really I don't.'

'Sure you do. You'd do the same, if you were in our position.'

Kate turned to go back inside the house, but then a thought struck her. 'Marie, is Patrick home?'

'I think so, why?'

'I need to ... I'll see you later. Bye.'

She left her friend open-mouthed on the doorstep and took the stairs two at a time. Once on the top floor, however, her resolve nearly left her. But she raised her hand and knocked sharply.

'Kate, is everything okay?'

'I was going to go for a walk and I wondered –'

'Did Sam like the TV?'

They both spoke at the same time, overlapping, then laughing nervously.

'You go first,' Patrick told her.

Kate swallowed. 'I was just saying that I'm going for a walk and I wondered whether you'd like to come.'

'Oh. Right.'

'If you're busy, it's no problem. Another time, maybe.'

'Kate. I'd love to. I'll get my coat.'

'Okay, then.' She smiled at his retreating back. It did feel better to be doing something. Much, much better.

Patrick returned, shrugging on a checked jacket. 'Off we go then.'

'Hang on a minute. Not so fast. You didn't tell me what it was you were going to say. Just then,' she prompted. 'When I talked over you.'

'Oh, right.' He looked awkward for a moment, and her heart tugged. There was something about this man. Something about the way his hair curled around the tops of his ears, the way he tipped his head down when he was nervous, and then peered out at her from under his furrowed brow. Something she just couldn't shake. 'I just wondered how it went with Sam.'

'I'll pay you for the TV,' she said quickly, turning at the top of the stairs to face him.

'Kate.' He took her hand and held it to his chest. 'Please don't worry about it. Tell me about Sam.'

She smiled to herself and let out a long sigh. 'Come on, then. Let's walk and talk. You won't believe how cute he is when he sleeps.'

***

Marie was waiting for them back at Bow Hill, and Kate's heart lurched at the sight of her hovering in the hallway, her thoughts turning immediately to Sam. But Marie had no news, was only excited to see them together, as she wasted no time in telling Kate once Patrick had headed out to work.

'He keeps odd hours,' Kate observed.

'He's his own boss out there in the woods,' Marie said, sighing with envy.

Marie had a new commission for Kate – another of her friends, a diminutive lady called Janice, wanted a tuxedo-style jacket for the Christmas season. Kate was pleased, if a little bemused.

'Christmas already? Isn't it a little early for that?'

'Kate!' Marie's hand flew up to her chest in alarm. 'I'm shocked at you. It is never too early to start thinking about Christmas.'

While Kate worked, Marie asked about Sam and the court case.

'What will happen now? I mean, does it make a difference to the guardianship thingy? With your dad ... Look, I'm being insensitive. Sorry.'

'No, it's okay. I've been thinking about that too. I don't want it to seem like I'm being heartless either,' Kate confessed, glancing up from her sewing with anxious eyes, 'but I am genuinely worried about my mother. We might have our differences –'

'And then some!' Marie put in.

'Quite. But she's not getting any younger. And Sam is hard work – all toddlers are.'

'She must be overwrought,' Marie agreed. 'If she weren't so hell bent on ruining your life I might feel sorry for her.'

Kate smiled, grateful for the gesture of loyalty. 'I don't know, Marie. I can't see a good ending to any of this. At first I was so upset, I thought that when I got Sam back I might never let her see him again. But I don't think I could do that to her, not now.'

'Despite all that she's done?'

'Because of all that she's done!' Kate sighed, registering the confusion on Marie's face. 'How can I hate someone who loves Sam so much she'd sacrifice everything to keep him? What kind of a hypocrite would that make me? I mean, if anyone can understand how she feels it's me. She deserves a bit of compassion.'

Bending over the sewing machine, Kate tried to hide the prickling of tears in her eyes. She felt the loss of her father like a corkscrew in her soul. She would never have the chance to hear him say sorry; never have the opportunity to heal the wounds that had festered for so many years.

'Well, she's lucky to have a daughter like you,' Marie said with a grimace. 'It's not long now, is it?'

'A week tomorrow,' Kate said, shaking her head. She glanced at the calendar on the wall, the red crosses marking her progress every step of the way. 'It still feels like a lifetime.'

'But it isn't. Three more visits with Sam, and then he'll be with you for good. And tomorrow we'll get his room painted, get those curtains up, make it all perfect for him.'

The curtains had brightly coloured ship motifs with pure white sails on a deep blue background and were folded neatly on top of a box of toys Kate had scavenged from the thrift shop. In Sam's room, the cot had been covered with a protective cloth in readiness, along with the armchair and a small chest of drawers donated by Marie.

While Marie was busy inspecting the clothes Kate had made for Sam, oohing and ahhing over each little outfit, Kate's gaze slid to the dress that hung on the back of her door, shrouded in a dry-cleaning cover to keep out prying eyes. It was the only way she could say thank you to her friend, and she couldn't wait to see Marie's face when it was finished.

'Will your ex be here to help with the decorating?' Marie said, standing and stretching out her back. Kate grimaced, and shook her head.

'I hope not.'

'Not with Patrick around, eh?' Marie said with a wink.

That wasn't the only reason, but Kate couldn't deny it was a factor. She glanced at her watch, then sighed.

'Speaking of Evan, I need to get ready. He's taking me out for a drink tonight. We arranged it last week.'

Marie's eyebrows shot up so high they nearly

disappeared into her hair.

'It's not what you're thinking,' Kate told her wearily. 'But I can't just ignore him, can I? He's Sam's dad, and he's here in Corrin Cove large as life. And I don't want him just turning up here whenever it suits him.'

'Because that really would cramp your style,' Marie finished, turning her eyes up towards the ceiling and treating Kate to another meaningful wink. Kate shook her head slowly, then turned away. There was no way she was going to admit to her friend how close to the mark her comment was.

Chapter 21

Kate managed an hour and a half with Evan before she felt compelled to go home. Sitting in a crowded bar listening to her ex recount his tales of misadventure, watching him get drunk while he pressed his knees against hers in the cramped space and grinned at her over the top of his pint, was not Kate's idea of a fun evening.

'I'll walk you home,' he slurred, and Kate was too exhausted to say no. Let him play the gentleman if he wanted. It could only help to get rid of him more quickly.

For most of the short walk back to Bow Hill, Evan sang at the top of his voice; it seemed he'd picked up some old sea shanty during his brief stay in Corrin Cove, and he insisted on regaling Kate with verse after verse of it, most of which she was sure he'd made up. But she was laughing in spite of herself by the time they reached her front door.

'Where are you staying, Evan?' Kate asked him as she fumbled in her bag for her key.

'TravelDen,' he said sourly. 'It's a dump.'

'My mother's budget doesn't stretch to the Grand Hotel on the seafront?'

Evan shook his head, evidently throwing himself off balance and veering against her, almost knocking them both into the road.

'Oops,' he said, stumbling back towards the wall.

'Well, thanks for the drink. Goodnight.' Kate let herself inside, but Evan was too quick for her. When she turned to close the door he was standing behind her in the hall.

'Coffee?' he said grinning.

'No, I really don't think that's ...'

Kate closed her mouth with a sigh. Evan was already halfway up the stairs, lurching from side to side as though he was on a ship at sea.

She glanced towards Marie's rooms, but there was no sign of her landlady. Evan peered down at her, shushing her loudly and gesturing for her to follow him up. Kate sighed again.

As soon as she let him inside, Evan flopped onto the bed, patting it in what he clearly thought was an inviting fashion. Kate shook her head.

'You can have your coffee, Evan, and then you can go.'

'Okay, Katie. If that's what you want.'

'And can you stop calling me Katie? You know it winds me up.'

She crossed the room, filling the kettle from the tap in the en suite. When she turned, Evan was standing in the doorway, blocking her path.

'Katie. Come and sit down.'

She pushed past him and set down the kettle, her instincts on red alert. Drunk or not, Evan was stronger than her, and he had that look in his eyes she knew so well.

He wanted her.

'Evan,' she began, but he shook his head, his unfocused eyes not leaving her face. He reached out his hand and put a finger to her lips. When he moved he moved quickly, pulling her roughly to the bed, pinning her underneath him.

'No,' she cried, but her voice was muffled against his

chest. He smelt of beer and sweat and stale aftershave, and a hot kind of energy. She couldn't think straight, could only feel the pressure of him pushing her down, could only see his eyes, hooded and glazed, bearing down over her.

She wriggled her arms out of his grip, heard him laugh as he mistook the wriggling for pleasure. His smug laughter gave her an idea.

'Wait,' she gasped, reaching up to place her hands on either side of his face. She kept her grip light, as though it was no more than a caring gesture. She smiled, and felt him ease off just slightly. 'Evan, there's no need to force me. Let's take it a little slower, okay?'

He peered down, his expression measuring. She gave a nod of encouragement, and suddenly his eyes cleared and he grinned.

'Ah, Katie. You don't change, do you? Still gagging for it, right? Can't get enough of your Evan.'

'You got it,' she said, fixing a smile to her face. He shifted to the edge of the bed. She lay unmoving, holding her breath.

'You know,' he said, getting up with effort and swaying into the middle of the room, 'all this is so pointless. You should be having a good time, not making these stupid clothes, sitting here sewing like an old granny. It was the same back in Manchester – you were so boring! And that bloody sailor outfit, I recognise that. Is it the same one or are you making another? It's like you're obsessed, woman.'

He lurched towards the en suite, pointing a finger at her over his shoulder. 'You stay right there little lady while I go take a slash. I'll be back,' he added with a salacious grin. 'You can start without me if you like.'

Kate waited until he closed the toilet door behind him. And then she was on her feet, moving faster than she'd ever moved before. Out of the door, up the stairs, her feet barely touching the worn carpet, her hands feeling the way in the half-light. There was Patrick's door, and she flung herself against it, rapping with her knuckles, all the while staring with wide eyes over her shoulder.

Patrick opened the door at once, and Kate stepped back, pointing shakily down the stairs. 'Evan,' she whispered. 'He's drunk, he's ...' she tailed off, unable to bring herself to say the words.

'Wait inside,' Patrick said, moving out of the way so Kate could edge past him silently. She watched him jog down to the first floor. He was barefoot and made no sound at all.

'Wait,' she hissed. 'I'm coming too.'

She tiptoed down after him, sliding her eyes away from his smooth, bare chest.

'Kate, you should–'

'No. I've had enough of standing by and letting things happen to me. I want to do this. But I need you for–'

'Backup?' Patrick offered. It was too dark to see his expression, but Kate thought he was smiling. She nodded.

'Backup. Right.'

When Evan came out of the en suite, zipping up his fly and whistling amiably, Kate was waiting for him. She had her phone in one hand and a pair of sewing scissors in the other.

'You need to leave now,' she told him, gesturing towards the open door. 'And I don't want to see you again. Not in court, not in Corrin Cove, and certainly not around Sam. Go back to Scotland or Manchester or wherever and get on with your life, Evan. Forget about us.'

He laughed, lurching towards her, then veering away in mock horror, hands raised, at the sight of the scissors.

'Or what? You'll sew me to death?'

Kate lifted her phone. 'It has voice dialling. If you attack me again I'll call the police.'

'Go ahead, Katie. I'm sure they'll be fascinated to visit this place. Oh, I see.' He nodded slowly. 'We're not alone anymore.'

Patrick lifted a hand in a half-wave, then returned to his relaxed pose leaning against the wall in the corridor outside. Kate's heart banged in her chest; she focused on her hand, determined not to let Evan see it shaking. For ten seconds, twenty seconds, no one moved. Then Evan laughed again.

'Hey, chill out, Katie. Take a compliment. So your old ex still fancies you, but I get it – you've moved on. No problem.' He strolled out onto the landing, tipping his head at Patrick. 'Jeez, the things people will do to get out of making a cup of coffee.'

Kate heard Marie come out into the hallway as Patrick saw Evan out of the house for the second time, heard a murmured conversation, and then the sound of Marie's door closing again. She shivered and hugged herself. It wasn't cold. Patrick appeared, climbing the stairs two at a time, and then he crossed the small landing and held her close to him, making no attempt to take her either into her room or up to his own. She could feel the warmth of his chest through her sweater, the tension in the arms that encircled her. She flicked her gaze to his mouth, then she closed her eyes, waiting, not waiting, not knowing what might happen next. And then his lips were on hers, gently, the very gesture a question needing to be asked. She responded by pulling him close, losing herself in his embrace, moulding her body to his. The beauty and sweetness of it overwhelmed her; she felt his kisses on her cheeks, her lips, her eyelids, kissing away her tears, chasing away the fear. Her need became stronger, and she pressed herself to him more firmly, exploring his mouth with her tongue.

And then he was pulling away, holding her at arms' length, his mouth blurred by their passion.

'I ... I'm sorry,' she said, touching her fingers to her lips as though she could still feel his kiss there.

'No, Kate, I'm sorry,' Patrick said. 'I shouldn't have ... It was taking advantage. I'm just as bad as –'

'You are not!' Kate cried, reaching out for him again. 'Don't ever say that. Evan was drunk, and won't take no for an answer at the best of times. I'm sorry for involving you, for waking you up, but please don't think that what just happened between us was anything like what Evan tried to do.'

But Patrick's expression told her he was far from convinced. 'You should get some sleep,' he said. 'We've got a busy day tomorrow.'

'You don't have to help with the painting if you don't want to,' Kate heard herself saying. 'I mean, you've already done so much. I wouldn't want to impose.'

'Impose?' He regarded her, his face impossible to read.

'I mean, if you're busy. I don't want to put you out.' Kate closed her mouth, unable to trust what might come out of it next. Her mind was still reeling from Evan's unwelcome pass at her, and from Patrick's very welcome embrace.

'Goodnight, Kate,' Patrick said softly. 'Call me if you hear from your ex again, or if there's anything else you need.'

Before Kate could think of what to say, Patrick had gone, and she was left alone on the landing, the darkness making all the edges fuzzy, her ears buzzing in the silence. She trudged back into her own room, closed and locked the door, and stood with her back pressed against it with her eyes closed for the longest time. And then she crossed the room, lay down on the bed, and fell into a deep and dreamless sleep.

Chapter 22

The glass felt cold in her fingers – ice-cold even though there was no ice. Maybe it was her hands that were cold. Barbara put the glass down and tucked her fists under her armpits. That was better. She rocked slightly in her chair, listening to the creak of the wood on the floorboards. She must get David to oil the bloody thing. She must tell him to …

Barbara stopped rocking and fixed her eyes on a point on the wall opposite. She allowed her thoughts to slip away, allowed her mind to shut down. This technique had been working well so far, and she saw no reason to stop using it now. Her friends, the endless dance of them through her house, kept telling her not to be afraid to let her feelings out. What did they know? What clue did they have with their perfect families, their married, sensible children, devoted husbands, perky grandkids? It made her sick to hear them going on and on. But the look on their faces when she had told them to get out of her house and leave her alone. That had been priceless.

Now she was alone. Well, not quite. Not yet. She still had Samuel. He was playing in David's study, building something on his granddad's desk with those everlasting bricks of his. For when Pops comes home, he'd said. Barbara had told him, she'd tried to explain it, but Samuel had merely looked up at her with those huge eyes of his and said, 'Don't be silly, Nana. Pops live here. He be home soon.'

Well, the boy would find out the truth soon enough. And it wasn't the only truth, either. She knew her days with him were numbered now but somehow, despite everything, she couldn't bring herself to believe it would really happen. He was all she had left. He was all she'd ever had.

She still had one ace up her sleeve. But she was far from sure whether it would work.

Damn David. Damn the lot of them.

Pushing the drink to one side, Barbara picked up the photo album that lay by her feet. Funny, because she had forgotten all about it until a few weeks ago when she found her husband searching frantically in the dresser. She never did find out what he was looking for; now she never would. She shook the thought away and opened the album. Page after page of holiday photos. Herself, Katherine and David in France, in Spain, Scotland, Wales, the Lake District. So Kate had had a terrible childhood, had she? These photographs told a different story. The child in these photographs was smiling; she was happy. She played in the sand and ate ice creams. She held her father's hand and carried a balloon, her face lit up like the sun.

Barbara wasn't in many of the photos, and at first she wondered why. It wasn't as if she were particularly camera-shy. But then she remembered: she had been the one taking the pictures. Which, in a way, made her even more present than the subjects. Without her the images wouldn't exist.

Just like David didn't exist anymore.

She forced herself to look closely at the image of her husband in the photograph she held now between her frozen fingers. At the way his hair swept to one side – oh, how he'd fought to keep hold of that parting even when it got bigger and bigger, and his hair thinner and thinner – and at his face, his eyes, his laughing mouth. Had that been before, she wondered? Before it all started to go wrong for them. Before he'd started to drink – not just for fun, like she did, but seriously, as though it was a job of work he needed to master. The drink had changed him, she knew that, but underneath he was always David. He always came back to her eventually.

He wasn't coming back to her now. And Barbara knew exactly who was to blame. The person who had taken away her happiness, her peace of mind, her husband. The person who was trying to take away her boy. She pulled the photo out of its plastic sleeve and held it carefully between her thumb and forefinger. With her other hand, she picked up the nail scissors and started to cut.

Chapter 23

If her sleep was devoid of the usual nightmares, Kate's waking hours the next day were not. From the moment the sun glared through the curtainless windows, pulling her from sleep with all the subtlety of a road digger, Kate's thoughts were plagued by memories of the night before. The maelstrom of emotions had left her feeling weak and vulnerable, unable to concentrate on the simplest task. Even her visit with Sam failed to soothe her mind. And when the session was over, and Kate had to once again kiss her son goodbye while all the other parents wrapped their children in warm coats and got them ready for lunch dates or took them home to play, she had felt more than ever that her heart would simply break from the pain of it. Her mother, resplendent in a cashmere coat and impeccably tied scarf, fresh from the salon with the smell of hairspray still clinging to her clothing, had smiled at Kate, and thrust a piece of paper into her shaking hand.

'The funeral,' she said, her gaze withering as she took in Kate's dishevelled appearance. 'It's on Monday if you can manage to come.'

'Of course I'll come,' Kate responded, but her mother was already walking away. Sam waved and shouted, 'Bye bye, Mummy!' but even that couldn't lift Kate's spirits. She walked slowly home, her head low, her mood even lower.

Back at Bow Hill, Patrick and Marie had made a start

on Sam's room, Patrick on a stepladder cutting in while Marie tackled the longest expanse of wall with a ratty-looking roller. Kate had chosen sky blue and spring green for the room, and the sight of the clean, bright colours cheered her a little. Patrick said hello and threw her a warm smile, which melted her insides but also sent her into a flurry of confusion.

'Do you fancy going out for something to eat later?' he asked when Marie popped downstairs to make coffee.

'Sorry,' Kate said automatically, 'I can't. I've really got a lot to do, sewing work and stuff, and I should be getting on with –'

'That's fine,' he said, smiling. The smile, however, did not reach his eyes. 'No worries.'

They worked on in silence, with a music station on the TV giving Marie the opportunity to show off her dancing moves, much to Kate's amusement. By mid-afternoon the painting was finished, and Kate stood back and nodded, satisfied.

'It looks great,' she said.

Marie clapped her hands in delight. 'I can't wait for little Sam to see it.'

'Neither can I,' Kate agreed. But then a sense of dread hit her from nowhere, pulling her down into its depths. Would he see it? Her mother had seemed so sure of herself today, smiling that secret smile. Almost as if she knew something Kate didn't. Well, of course it must be to do with Evan. No doubt he'd told Barbara about Kate's rejection, and now he would be all set to do his worst at the court hearing. She wondered whether Evan would be at her father's funeral, perhaps as her mother's guest, and she wondered how Sam would get through it, whether he'd even understand what was going on.

'Penny for them,' Marie said, putting her arm around Kate's shoulder after Patrick had packed up the stepladders and said goodbye.

'He's upset with me,' Kate mused.

'Is that why you have a face like a wet weekend?' Marie asked, wiping her paint-splattered hands on her overalls. She gathered together the makeshift dust sheets and threw them over her shoulder. 'I'll pop these out on the landing, get Patrick to put them back in the loft later. For what it's worth, Kate, I don't think he's upset with you. He likes you, I'm sure. But you've been through a lot. You've just lost your dad, you're going through a custody battle, and then there's Evan ... Patrick probably doesn't know how to play it, that's all.'

He's not the only one, Kate thought, but she said nothing.

'Coffee?' Marie asked, and Kate nodded gratefully. She looked around the room, enjoying being alone, taking in the way the colours reflected the slanted light, the way the blue of Sam's new curtains complemented the blue of the walls. He would be happy here.

She picked up Sam's new sailor suit and smiled. And then her expression soured, recalling Evan's barbed jibe. He had a nerve. What had he said exactly? It had been niggling at her all day, this sense of something waiting on the edges of her memory, ready to fall into place like a key turning the mechanism of a well-oiled lock.

Evan had asked her whether Sam's sailor suit was the same one she'd made in Manchester. It hadn't registered at the time, but now Kate realised what it was that had been bothering her.

Evan had left her and Sam months before she'd even started on that sailor suit. There was no way he could have known about it, no way at all. She remembered his disdain last night, how he'd accused her of being obsessed. An old granny, sitting at her sewing machine, day in, day out. And he was right – that was exactly what she had become, both here and back at her flat in Manchester before the break-in. Before the knock to her head that had left her unconscious.

The knock to her head that had caused her to lose a year of her life, not to mention her son.

If Evan had seen the sailor suit in Manchester, he must have been in her flat at some point after the time when her mother came to stay. She hadn't started making clothes for Sam until after that; she hadn't started work on the sailor suit until she'd found those special buttons and got the idea out of a magazine.

Had her mother told him about Sam's outfit? Was that possible? Kate couldn't imagine any conversation where that might come up. Maybe she had seen Evan but didn't remember. No. She shook her head so violently her hair whipped back and forth, flicking her in the face. No way. She would remember. With Sam still in nappies, with her whole life one long struggle from one meal to the next, one sleep to the next, Kate knew that Evan would not have been a welcome guest in her home at any point after he'd abandoned her.

So how did he know about the sailor suit she'd made for Sam?

She pressed her head against the cold glass of the window and closed her eyes. The nightmare came back to her, making her shiver. That sense of someone standing behind her when she knew there should be no one there. The fear she felt, like insects crawling over her body. Sam, playing in his pen, cooing at her, chewing on a toy. He was teething. She remembered that now, and the realisation that this was a new memory, a brand new detail, jolted through her like an electric current. Yes, Sam had been teething. She hadn't slept for two nights and she was bone tired. She could see her old flat in her mind's eye, the washing on the drainer, the sterilising bowl overflowing with bottles and teats. The couple in the flat below were arguing again, and Kate was tired of listening to them. She had flopped down at the table with her head in her hands and let the tears of exhaustion fall. She was tired of everything, tired of being tired. Sam gurgled and dropped his toy – a plastic tractor. It had clattered to the floor and made her jump.

And then Kate had sat up, suddenly alert. Something else had caught her attention, but what? A creak of a floorboard where it shouldn't have creaked? She remembered sitting there at the table, alert to the very movement of the air around her. And she had felt it then, the sense of being watched. The sense of time standing still, the ticking of a clock, the muffled arguing below. A smell, alien to that space; not the smell of Sam's dirty nappies or washing drying on radiators or the acrid scent that crept into her flat when the boy next door smoked out of his window.

It was the smell of danger. And she had smelt it again last night, right here in her room in Bow Hill.

Kate placed her hands on the glass now, palms flat, spreading her fingers wide. In her mind she sent herself back to her nightmare, willing the scene into life. Turn around, she said silently. Don't be afraid, Kate. Turn around and see who it is.

She already knew who she would see there.

When she opened her eyes again the light in her room had all but gone and her own pale face stared back at her from the window. Reflected in the ghostly glass, her room was bare, just a bed and a table. No playpen here. No Sam. But then a movement behind her caught her eye and she spun around, crying out in alarm, her hand flying up to her mouth.

It was only Marie's dress, hanging from the door, swaying slightly in a draught from the badly fitting window. Kate sat down on her bed, her heart banging, her mind suddenly alive with answers.

Chapter 24

'Madam, slow down. I can't understand what you're saying.'

Kate took a deep breath and pressed the phone closer to her ear.

'I need to speak to PC Georgia Mayer. Please – it's absolutely imperative I speak to her at once.'

'Imperative, is it? Absolutely.' The Mancunian accent made a mockery of Kate's efforts to sound important.

'Look, is PC Mayer there? She was dealing with my case last year, it was a robbery, I mean a burglary – I don't know exactly what you'd call it. My flat was broken into and I was attacked. I was hit over the head and I was in a coma for a year, well about nine months to be exact, and I had no idea who did it but now I do. And I need to tell her. I need to tell someone right away.'

'Well, why don't you tell me and I'll pass the message on.'

'No! I want to talk to someone now. I know who it was, and he's here in Corrin Cove right now and he's going to speak up for my mum at the hearing and then no one will believe me …'

Kate stopped. She was babbling. She needed to get a grip.

'Do you believe yourself to be in danger at this precise moment, madam?'

'No,' Kate said sullenly, looking around her sunlit bedroom and feeling a little silly.

'I see. And when you say that the perpetrator is in Cobbit Cove right now, what does that mean exactly?'

'Corrin Cove,' Kate corrected. 'It's near St Austell. Near Plymouth,' she added, painfully aware of how small and insignificant her tiny town would seem to the police in a metropolis like Manchester.

'Oh, Plymouth,' the sergeant said, as though that explained everything.

After a couple more tries, Kate left a message for whoever was still dealing with her case and rang off. She'd given them Evan's full name – surely when they looked at his record they would put two and two together and ring her right back. But after half an hour she realised it wasn't going to happen. At least, it wasn't going to happen as quickly as she hoped.

Meanwhile, she had a funeral to go to. She just hoped she wouldn't have to face Evan there.

***

It was the perfect day for a funeral. Low clouds gave the sky a heavy, portentous appearance and a dusting of rain forced the mourners to cluster together in little groups under the shelter of their umbrellas.

The sight of the umbrellas came close to producing a smile on Kate's face, although it never actually materialised. Most of them were regulation black but a few, most likely grabbed from cars at the last minute, were outrageously bright and colourful. An oversized one with green and white stripes tilted merrily in the wind amongst a sea of black. And another, pink and purple check, cast a rosy glow over the faces of the two women huddled underneath.

Kate let the half-smile drop from her face as the coffin appeared, shouldered by four men from her father's golf club and two solemn-faced employees of the funeral director. She held on to Marie's arm even tighter as the box reached the side of the grave and was lowered slowly into the hole, thankful for her friend's physical and moral support. Thank goodness Sam wasn't here to see this. At least that was something her mother had got right, leaving him with friends for the day. Although maybe it would have helped him to say goodbye to his granddad. Selfishly, Kate would have given anything to have her son by her side right now, to feel his little hand in hers.

'Not long now,' Marie murmured, and Kate threw her a grateful glance.

The vicar spoke in a monotone which failed to carry over the wind, and the sound of traffic from the main road at the north edge of the graveyard drowned him out even further. Kate was glad she couldn't hear him. The words he had spoken inside the church told of a man she had never even known: a pillar of the community, a cheerful soul, loved and respected by everyone he met. So her father had been a generous man, a hard worker, well-regarded and widely liked by a host of people she'd never seen before. They'd crowded the church, seeking out her mother to speak in hushed tones of concern and grief. Kate was touched and hurt in equal measure. How she wished she had known the man they had.

Her mother was an ice-maiden, and Kate didn't know whether to be impressed by her calm stoicism or embarrassed by her coldness. The woman was immaculately dressed as usual, hair perfectly styled and freshly coloured, nails sharp little half-moons of pink when she removed her calf-skin gloves. She made Kate feel like an unwashed tramp – albeit from a distance.

If any of the mourners knew that David had a daughter, or that she was here right now in their midst, they didn't show it. Kate was more grateful than ever that she had Marie by her side. Her friend was a rock throughout the service, and now she helped Kate keep her emotions in check as they stood outside in the rain, watching the vicar commit her father to the earth.

It was only then that Kate allowed herself to cry. She cried for the father she wished she'd had, and for the one who had hurt her so badly. She took the perfumed hanky Marie held out and pressed it to her eyes, her nose, covering her face to hide the sight of the soil that was now being shovelled on top of the pale wooden coffin. It landed with a thump and Kate winced at the sound.

She turned away, unable to watch any longer, and came face to face with her mother.

'Mum.'

'Kate.'

At close range Barbara's face was far from the groomed picture of perfection it had appeared to be from a distance. Lines bracketed her mouth, and her eyes were swollen slits, their blue turned to black under the darkening sky.

'Mum, are you okay?' Kate shook her head. Stupid question. 'Listen,' she said quickly. 'I need to talk to you. It's about Evan.'

'Not now,' her mother said under her breath, and she turned away sharply.

'I remembered,' Kate called, hurrying after her. 'I remembered what happened the night of the attack. Mum, it was Evan. You can't trust him. You mustn't ... Mum, where are you going?'

Most of the mourners had drifted away from the graveside, but a few lingered, trying to look as though they weren't listening to the exchange, although they clearly were. Kate felt her face grow hot with embarrassment. She glanced at Marie, who was opening and closing her mouth like a goldfish. Then she noticed a figure striding across the graveyard, his face like a beacon in the greying afternoon.

'Am I glad to see you,' Marie hissed, throwing a dark look over her shoulder to where Barbara stood, outlined against the sky like a statue.

'I only just got your message,' Patrick said, steering them past the worst of the puddles onto the gravel path. 'I'd have come sooner if I'd known.' He glanced at Kate, and she saw the hurt there, naked and exposed, although he quickly altered his expression back to one of concern.

'I'm sorry,' she said. 'I only told Marie this morning.'

I had one or two other things on my mind, she thought. 'I'm glad you came, though,' she said. 'Really glad. To both of you. Thank you for being here for me.'

Marie squeezed her arm, then told her to get a move on. 'This rain isn't doing anything for my frizzy hair.'

Kate allowed herself to breathe again, tilting her face up to the sky and letting the rain cool her skin. This was not the day for a confrontation, not the time to expose the truth about Evan to her mother. Emotions were running too high all round.

But when they reached the car, Kate turned to see her mother doggedly following, a look of grim determination shadowing her face. Patrick had already got into the driver's seat and was waiting for Kate to join him. She bent her head to his half-open window. 'I have to deal with this. Hang on a minute.'

'So what new lies are you cooking up now?' Barbara said quietly, glancing back over her shoulder at the churchyard. 'Have you no shame?'

Kate shook her head and looked at her mother sadly. 'It's not a lie, Mum. Evan slipped up. He saw something in my flat, my old flat, something he could only have seen if he'd been there after he'd already left. Once I'd realised ...' She lifted her shoulders and dropped them. 'It all came back to me. I know it was him because it was him. I remember.'

The rain had drenched Kate's face so completely that

175

she hadn't even noticed she was crying, and it was a surprise now to find the tears falling from her eyes with no effort at all. Kate saw that her mother's face was also soaked, the heavy make-up washed away in streaks of black and brown. Despite all that has happened, Kate thought, she is still my mother.

'Why don't we go back to my place and talk about all this properly?' she said. 'We're both getting drenched here and it's really cold.'

Barbara shook her head violently.

'Mum, don't be–'

'Are you sure?' She gripped Kate's arm with surprising strength. 'Are you sure it was him?' Kate nodded. Her mother appeared to slump in on herself, and then she whispered something under her breath before turning and walking unevenly back towards the church.

As they drove away, Kate watched in the rear-view mirror. She watched her mother recede further and further, until she was out of sight completely.

Chapter 25

'Hi, little man,' Kate said, bending down to kiss the top of Sam's head. Would she ever get tired of the feel of his hair on her face, of his special, sweet smell? They settled into their usual visit routine, and Sam chattered to her constantly as he played, crawling in and out of an indoor tepee, bringing Kate pretend meals and books to read. She loved the sound of his voice, loved letting it wash over her like a cleansing bath of sound. Even now she could remember the exact pitch of each of his cries as a baby. From day one she had instinctively known what each cry meant.

When his chatter stopped suddenly, Kate looked up and followed his gaze out through the centre's reception area to where her mother was standing, staring into space.

'Are you okay?' Kate asked him.

He twisted away, averting his face. 'Nana sad,' he said, so quietly she had to strain to hear him.

'Is she?' Kate thought for a moment, flicking her eyes back her mother, then down to where her son sat, chewing on his fingers. 'Would you like me to talk to her?' she asked him. Sam nodded and smiled broadly. He grabbed hold of Kate's hand and gave it a sloppy kiss.

'Mummy kiss it better,' he said, glancing back out to reception.

Much good it will do, Kate thought, but she promised to give it a try.

'Sam, before I go today there's something I need to tell you.'

He looked at her expectantly. Trustingly.

'The thing is, sweetie, both your nana and I love you very much. You know that, right?' He nodded, his eyes enormous in his solemn little face. 'And you know that you've been living with her for a while now. While I was ...'

'You were asleep,' Sam told her. 'Like Sleeping Beauty.'

Kate stopped and stared at him. 'That's right, Sam. What a lovely way to think of it.'

'Pops told me. He said you were under a spell, but that you woke up and came back.'

Kate swallowed hard. She took a deep breath and tried to focus. 'Well, that was very kind of Pops. And, as he said, I'm back now. I woke up and now I'm back. So how would you like it if you came to live with me for a while? Only if you wanted to. Only if you liked it, Sam.'

He regarded her carefully, weighing it up. She waited, her breath caught in her chest.

'Bring my bricks?' he said.

'Of course,' Kate gushed eagerly. 'You can bring whatever you want. And we'll visit Nana, and you can still see all your friends. It will be like an adventure. Okay?'

He shrugged and nodded. 'Okay.'

Kate sighed in relief. One hurdle over. Now it was time to tackle the next one.

'You wait here for a moment, sweetie. I'm just going to go and talk to Nana.'

Barbara greeted her coolly, and Kate had the feeling she'd been watching them the whole time, despite her distant stare.

'Sam wanted me to talk to you. He said you were sad.'

'Under the circumstances that's hardly surprising, is it?'

'Mum,' Kate said softly, 'can't we sort this out? It's not too late. Nothing has been done that can't be undone.'

'Can you bring your father back from the dead?'

Kate looked away. 'Of course not.'

'Evan's gone. I thought you'd need to ... I thought you'd want to tell the police. I have his address here. The one he had in Scotland.'

Kate took the folded sheet of paper and looked at it. 'Thank you. This means a lot to me.'

'It doesn't change anything, Kate.'

'Doesn't it?'

'Some things can't be undone.'

Barbara's voice seemed to catch in her throat. Kate looked up in surprise. She tried to see her mother's expression, but the light was behind her, throwing her face into shadow.

Chapter 26

Barbara was staring out of the window, lost in thought, when Samuel toddled into the dining room, rubbing his stomach. He asked about dinner and Barbara looked at him in surprise. She had forgotten about dinner, forgotten about food entirely. She held out her arms to him and he climbed up onto her lap.

'When Pops home?' he asked, his voice muffled against her blouse.

'Not for a while,' she told him gently. What else could she say? She had tried so hard to explain but the words never seemed to come out right. The truth was, she could hardly believe it herself. The man had been such a huge presence that the house seemed shrunken without him. It also seemed far more run-down than she'd ever noticed before. Now, the list of jobs and repairs was already starting to crowd her mind and make her feel weary to her bones.

'Hungry,' Samuel said.

Barbara sighed and placed him on the floor where he looked with interest at the photos Barbara still hadn't put away.

'Who that?' he said, pointing to the disembodied head of Kate aged eight years old.

'No one,' she said sharply. Samuel looked up in alarm. Barbara turned away, not liking what she saw in his face. Kate had looked at her like that sometimes –

afraid but also accusing, her young mind already forming judgments, or so it had seemed to Barbara. She bent down stiffly to gather up the pieces, and then told Samuel to go upstairs and wash for dinner.

'Come too?' he said hopefully.

'Go on, now.' She made a shooing motion with her hands

'Want Pops!' he cried, his voice turning into a wail.

'Please, Samuel,' Barbara said, pushing him away. 'Not now.'

The boy trudged out of the room, and soon she heard his sullen footsteps as he climbed the stairs. She looked at the half empty glass making a ring on her polished table and considered filling it up again. But as she got to her feet the floor seemed to tilt, and she realised that she was in fact very slightly drunk. She grabbed the glass and held it to the wall.

'Cheers, David!' she said, hearing the slurring of her words. 'Cheers, you old bastard. Thanks for leaving me on my own, for bailing out just when I needed you. You had to have the last laugh, didn't you? Same as always.'

She slumped back into the rocking chair and downed the rest of the gin and tonic in one swallow. The doctor had been less than half her age – younger than Kate, even. He'd said that her husband had known he was getting worse but had chosen not to tell anyone. Surely he would have told his own wife. Barbara couldn't make sense of it. A picture of her daughter sprang into her mind, huddled in the waiting room with those two rag-tag friends of hers – that woman, embodying mutton dressed as lamb, and the man, the way he'd looked at Kate, the way his eyes followed her around the room ...

'Nana. Nana! I stuck.'

Samuel's voice pierced her thoughts. She gazed at the ceiling – where was he? Oh, yes. Washing his hands. Stuck?

'Nanaaaaa!'

Barbara heaved herself out of the chair, calling to Samuel to wait for her. The stair gate must have accidentally closed behind him on his way up. She'd been telling David to take the blasted thing out for weeks – Samuel could manage the stairs fine now, he was so much more advanced than other children his age.

'Nana, look at me.'

'Samuel, no! Get down from there at once.' Barbara lurched across the hall, reaching blindly for her grandson. Samuel was balanced on top of the gate, one chunky leg on either side, waving his arms like a windmill.

'Weee, Nana,' he called, laughing in delight. 'Look at me. I can fly.'

Chapter 27

'How did it go this morning?'

Kate looked up from her sewing to see Marie standing in the doorway, bearing coffee.

'I keep getting this feeling of déjà vu,' she joked, smiling at Marie's puzzled expression. 'You, bringing me coffee and asking how I am. It's becoming rather a habit.'

'Oh, right.' Marie looked around for somewhere to set the tray, then put it down on the floor. 'Having a sort out?'

Kate's room was indeed a mess, with photographs and paperwork scattered over every surface, piles of clothes on the bed, and at least three unfinished sewing projects hanging up at various intervals around the walls.

'I'm trying to get on top of things, that's all.'

'Ready for Friday?'

Kate nodded. 'Whatever happens, I want to be ready.'

Marie hugged her coffee cup and offered Kate a chocolate biscuit. 'What will you do if you don't, I mean if it doesn't … If things don't work out the way you want them to?'

Kate looked up sharply. 'If I don't get my parental rights restored, you mean? Well, there's not much I can do, is there? But I'd like to stay on here, if that's okay with you. The court will still give me access to Sam, and he'll come and stay here whenever he can. And when he's older ...' She regarded her friend for a moment. 'This isn't like you, Marie. You're usually so upbeat about it. Have you changed your mind? Do you think I won't get Sam back now?'

Both Marie and Patrick had been quiet since the funeral, Patrick keeping himself to himself and Marie only appearing once a day with coffee, and only staying for a short time to chat. Whenever Kate let herself into the house she expected to see Marie popping out of her room like one half of a weather clock, but since Monday she'd been strangely absent.

'No, that's not what I meant,' Marie said, rubbing her eyes. 'I'm sure it will all work out fine. No court in the land is going to deny that you're perfectly fit to look after your own son.'

Kate wished she felt as confident. But she smiled and told Marie about her visit with Sam, and how comfortable he seemed with the idea of coming to live with her.

'That's nice.' Marie's voice was flat, devoid of inflection. Kate looked at her more closely, then she pushed back from the sewing table and came to sit by her side.

'What's up, Marie?'

'Nothing. The sky? I don't know, is it a trick question?'

'Good try at throwing me off, but I know you. Something's upset you.'

Marie sighed, long and heavy. 'It's Big Tony. He wants to take me out tonight. You know that new Chinese on the promenade? Well, he wants us to go there. He asked me on Monday, said he'd booked a table and everything. Tonight's our anniversary, you see. I mean, it would have been our anniversary if we hadn't got divorced.'

'That's really sweet.'

'Hmm.' Marie looked down at her hands, her face a picture of dejection.

'I'm missing something here, aren't I?' Kate mused. 'So, a date at a swanky new restaurant, an anniversary celebration. And that's making you sad because…?'

'Because,' Marie cried, 'he's either going to propose to me or break up with me, that's why!' She jumped up off the bed, dislodging two of the piles of clothes Kate had spent the morning sorting. 'Sorry,' she said, throwing them back onto the bed haphazardly. Kate got hold of her hands and made her sit down again.

'Marie, leave it. Now, what do you mean, propose or break up with you? What kind of crazy talk is that?'

'He only ever takes women to restaurants when he wants to get married to them or break up with them.' Marie imparted this information as though it was the most obvious thing in the world.

'I see,' Kate said, although she didn't see at all. She wondered yet again what the draw was with Big Tony, and why a sensible, vibrant woman like Marie was so hung up on him in the first place. But then she saw the agony in her friend's eyes, and decided it was none of her business. 'So,' she said, 'it's one or the other. And you have absolutely no idea which?'

'I think maybe … the first one?' Marie said in a small voice.

'Okay. And you're unhappy about that? Happy about that? Not sure?'

'Happy.' Marie jumped up again, yanking at her clothes and pulling a disgusted face. 'But look at me, Kate! I'm old and past it. I'm wrinkly and frumpy and the very idea is just ridiculous. There's no way I can go to a fancy-schmancy restaurant with him – as soon as he sees me in that context he'll surely realise that he can do better, and then he'll change his mind and choose the second option.'

'First of all,' Kate said, pulling Marie over to the mirror, 'you are not old, or past it, or wrinkly and frumpy. And he can not do better than you.' She bit her lip and wondered whether to risk her next comment. 'He should know, right? He's tried to replace you enough times.'

'You can say that again,' Marie laughed.

Relieved, Kate told her friend to close her eyes.

'What? Why would I do that?'

'Because I said so,' Kate said firmly. She crossed the room and pulled the yellow silk dress from its cover. She'd had to guess Marie's size, but she thought she'd done a pretty good job. She carried the dress over to Marie and held it up against her. 'Open your eyes,' she said.

Marie peered into the mirror, her gaze skimming up and down, her expression turning from puzzled to admiring and then back to puzzled again.

'Did you make this out of those old curtains of my grandma's?'

Kate nodded. 'You don't mind, do you? You said you'd like it if they were put to good use. And I thought the yellow would set off your hair perfectly. Be honest – do you like it? It's fine if you don't.'

'Like it? I love it! But ... are you saying this is for me?'

'Of course it's for you.'

'But I can't take this.'

'It didn't cost anything. You gave me the fabric yourself.' Kate laughed at her friend's expression. 'Just go and try it on, okay? Decide if you like it after you've tried it on.'

Still protesting, Marie allowed herself to be manoeuvred downstairs and into her room.

'I'll wait out here,' Kate called from the hallway. She grinned. It felt so good to be able to do something nice for someone else. She dug her bare toes into the carpet and waited. 'You'll knock Big Tony dead in that,' she shouted. 'He won't be able to resist you.'

She heard Marie call something back, but couldn't hear what it was. A knock at the door made her jump a little, and she turned to open it, still laughing to herself. Standing on the pavement, braced against the slope of Bow Hill, was Elizabeth.

'Oh, hi,' Kate began, but then she saw that the social worker was accompanied by a uniformed policeman, and that both of their faces were grave. 'Is it Sam?' she asked at once, her smile turning to ice in an instant.

Elizabeth shook her head. 'Sam's fine, Kate. This has nothing to do with him.'

Nothing to do with Sam? Then what ...

'Oh, right,' Kate said, nodding vigorously, suddenly understanding. 'You're here about Evan. Well, you took your time.' She addressed the grim-faced police officer, who looked to be no more than about eighteen, with pale skin and a patchy beard and skinny, sloping shoulders. 'I was expecting a phone call, but this is better. It will be easier for me to explain in person.'

She stood back to let them in. The officer looked at Elizabeth, who shrugged and followed him inside.

'Kate, it's amazing! Look at me – I'm a goddess.' Marie twirled into the hallway, nearly knocking the policeman against the wall. 'Oops,' she said, giggling. 'Sorry. Just having a bit of a fashion show here.'

'Marie, they've come about Evan.' Kate smiled, and gave her friend the thumbs up. 'You look amazing. Have a great time tonight. I'll tell you all about it tomorrow.'

'Kate,' Elizabeth said, stepping forward and laying a hand on her arm, 'I think you should be careful what you say.'

'But it's only Marie,' Kate said, laughing. 'I tell her everything.'

'No, but this officer has –'

'I have a warrant to search the premises of a Miss Kate Steiner,' the officer said, and his tone was so pompous that Kate almost laughed again. But then she processed his words, her eyes narrowing as she looked from him to Elizabeth, and finally to Marie.

'What did he say?' she asked, directing the question to the one person who looked the most puzzled of them all.

'He had a phone call,' Elizabeth began, but the policeman cut her off again.

'We received information yesterday to the effect that a Miss Kate Steiner of this address is in possession of a Class A drug, and I now have a warrant to search these premises to ascertain the exact –'

'Drugs!' shrieked Marie, throwing her hands into the air.

Kate shook her head slowly. No, she thought. This must be some kind of joke.

'You've got me mixed up with someone else,' she told him, but Elizabeth shook her head.

'When they looked you up on their database they found out about the court case and contacted me. I said I'd come along to ... To be here in case you need support.'

To see for myself, was what Elizabeth had been about to say, Kate was sure of it. She searched the other woman's face, but all she saw was a wary coolness.

'It isn't true,' Kate said. 'You're wasting your time, but go ahead and search my room. You won't find anything.'

'The warrant isn't only for your room, Miss Steiner. Our source said you are close friends with the other residents here. We'll be searching their rooms as well.'

'My room as well!'

'I'm sorry, Marie.' Kate threw a furious glare at the police officer. 'I'm sure it won't take long.'

188

'But I have ... personal things in there,' Marie whispered.

'Like what?'

'Artwork.' Marie pulled a face and opened her eyes wide. 'Big Tony – he likes to, you know, draw me. And stuff.'

'Oh.' Kate didn't know what to say. Her friend's reticence to allow her into her private space made sense now, but there wasn't much she could do to protect Marie's privacy in the face of a search warrant.

'We'll start with your room, Miss Steiner,' the officer said, and he stood to the side to let her pass, indicating that she should lead the way.

'Who made the phone call?' Kate asked Elizabeth, who began to trudge up the stairs behind her.

'I don't know.'

'Not that you'd tell me if you did.'

'I believe it was anonymous.'

Kate laughed bitterly. 'I'm not an idiot. Obviously it was my mother. Trying to muddy the waters again. She must be getting desperate if she'd stoop this low.'

'Have you spoken to your colleague in Manchester?' Kate asked the officer when they reached the top of the stairs. 'You know all about the attack, right? That I was unconscious, that I was in hospital for months?'

'I'm aware of the unresolved matter of an amount of cannabis that was found in your flat a year ago, yes,' he answered. He gestured towards the door. 'In there?'

Kate nodded mutely. She made to follow but he barred her way.

'If you'd just wait out here, Miss Steiner,' he said. And then he closed the door in her face.

Kate turned on Elizabeth, her eyes flashing fire. 'How could you let her do this? Don't you see what's going on here?'

'They got a phone call, Kate, and they have to –'

'But he wouldn't be here, would he, if not for the other drugs? You don't just go dashing off to get a search warrant based on one anonymous phone call. But you know that had nothing to do with me, you said so yourself. That first day, when I arrived here to see Sam, you told me you were on my side.'

'What I actually said was that I am on Sam's side,' Elizabeth told her calmly.

'Well,' Kate said, thinning her lips in disgust, 'sooner or later you are going to realise that they both mean the same thing.' She drummed her foot on the floor, wondering what her mother was doing right now. Probably sitting at home rubbing her hands together in delight.

'You said something about Evan downstairs,' Elizabeth said. 'About something you'd remembered?'

'Like you care,' Kate snapped. 'And if you had your finger on the pulse the way you should, you'd know that I reported it to the police two days ago. Yes, I remembered. It was Evan who attacked me and left me for dead. He wasn't in Scotland – he was right there, large as life. And I have proof,' she added, interpreting Elizabeth's expression as one of scepticism. 'He made a slip-up. He mentioned something of Sam's that he could only have seen if he was in the flat long after he'd left us. And I never once let him in willingly, so clearly he was up to no good. Evan knew I had some jewellery that was worth a bit of money, and he knew where I hid the little bit of cash I'd managed to save. It was him who ransacked the place, right after he knocked me out.'

'I see.'

Kate glanced at Elizabeth warily. The woman was so damned closed-off. It was impossible to know what she was thinking.

'It really was him. I'm certain of it. As soon as Evan mentioned Sam's sailor suit it all began to fall into place.

The doors of my memory ... they just sort of flew open.'

Elizabeth nodded. 'You're right. It would happen like that. And the nightmares you've been having?'

'I finally turned around,' Kate said simply. 'And there was Evan. I guess when I saw him there, in my flat, I flew at him and we argued. And this time, his temper took him too far. He must have panicked when I blacked out. Panicked and run away.'

'It makes sense, when you think about it,' Elizabeth said. 'He didn't hurt Sam, didn't touch anything of his. Not even in his room. That was always something that bothered me about your case.'

'That's true.' Kate hadn't thought about this before, and her blood ran cold just thinking about what might have happened to Sam if the intruder had been someone other than his own father.

'But, Kate, if it was Evan who hit you, then it must have been him who –'

'Hid the drugs in my flat, I know. I've been thinking about that. I think he must have broken in before, when Sam and I were out, and hidden them there. Maybe he was sleeping rough, wanted somewhere safe to put them. He left his key when he walked out on us, but of course he could have had a spare cut that I never knew about. I think he came back to get them, maybe he had a deal or something, couldn't wait until we went out again.' Kate laughed, but there was no humour in her voice when she said, 'Of course, we rarely went out anymore. I was so depressed I could hardly think straight.'

Elizabeth didn't speak for a minute. Kate looked at the door to her room and wondered what was taking so long. Elizabeth followed her gaze.

'Kate, has Evan ever been here? I mean, have you ever left him alone in your room?'

'No. Well, not really. Only that first time when he turned up and I was out, and the other day when he tried to ... He went into the bathroom, and I –'

She swallowed. 'He was only on his own for a few minutes.'

'A few minutes is all that it would take.'

Kate's hand flew up to her mouth as she realised what Elizabeth was saying.

'You don't think that he –?'

The door to her room swung open and the police officer stepped out, holding up a clear plastic bag with a triumphant flourish.

'Miss Steiner,' he said, 'I'm going to have to ask you to accompany me to the police station. There are one or two things we need to discuss.'

'Kate?'

Marie was standing on the stairs clutching the house phone to her chest. Her face was ashen, the yellow silk dress incongruous against her devastated expression. 'Kate, there's a call for you. It's the hospital. It's about ... Kate, it's Sam.'

Chapter 28

'She was drunk.'

Kate stated it flatly, keeping her hands locked together on her lap, her eyes fixed on the wall opposite. Back in the same hospital, only days after she'd been here for her father. And look what had happened to him.

Elizabeth shook her head. 'I don't think so. The paramedics didn't say–'

'I could smell it on her. I could see it in her eyes.'

'She wasn't drunk, Kate. It was an accident. Samuel tried to climb over the stair gate. There was nothing she could do. It happens. It's a lot more common than you might think.'

Kate shuddered, thinking how much worse it could have been. This time it was only a broken arm, but what about the next time? 'He shouldn't have been coming downstairs on his own in the first place. If she'd been caring for him properly–'

'Okay, fine.' Elizabeth stood and scraped back her chair. The waiting area was quieter now than when they'd first arrived, but the few people seated nearby glanced up at the social worker's exasperated sigh. 'You don't know what happened because you weren't there, but you're going to think the worst of her because that's how it is between you two. Frankly, I'm sick of it. She's breaking her heart over this, she feels so bad about it. But you know best, Kate. I'm going to get a drink.'

Kate watched her cross the waiting area, then she

jumped up and followed, weaving around the chairs, nearly tripping over a rucksack someone had dropped between two rows of plastic chairs.

She found Elizabeth by the coffee machine, blowing into a cardboard cup.

'I'm sorry,' she said. 'It's just hard to keep perspective.'

Elizabeth sipped her drink and said nothing.

'Is she?' Kate asked. 'Is my mother breaking her heart?'

'What do you think? She didn't get to him in time, she had to watch him fall. She said the sound of him screaming was like–'

'I should have been there!'

'You shouldn't have stormed off when your mother tried to explain to you what happened.'

'No.' Kate bit her lip and nodded. 'You're right. That was immature. I was angry at her, and scared. Scared for Sam.'

'So, you'll talk to her?' Elizabeth looked at Kate over the rim of her cup, one eyebrow raised. 'Like a grown-up?'

'Elizabeth, it's what I've been trying to do all along. But first,' Kate said, turning back in the direction of the wards, 'I need to check on Sam.'

***

Bones. White and smooth. Holding you together, but still so fragile. Breakable. On the X-ray, Sam's bones had been translucent and glowing, the fracture disturbingly distinct. His broken arm was encased in a plaster cast now, with just his chubby wrist poking out of the end, his hand palm up, fingers splayed, the way they had been during sleep when he was a baby. Kate stroked his cheek but he didn't wake up. He was exhausted, poor lamb. At least the painkillers were working.

She glanced up at a movement in the doorway.

Her mother edged into the room uncertainly. She held Sam's favourite teddy. She must have gone home to get it.

Kate returned her gaze to her son.

'He's such a brave boy,' her mother said. 'I was so proud of him.'

Kate said nothing. She brushed a stray hair from Sam's face, watching his eyelids flicker in the safety of sleep.

'Kate, I–'

'Mum, just leave it, okay? Elizabeth's explained what happened. I know it wasn't your fault. Sam will be fine. Let's just ... Look, I've had a hell of a day. Do you think we could just sit for a while? Just not talk?'

Barbara nodded mutely and tucked her chin into her neck. Kate allowed her shoulders to drop. She wondered what was happening at the police station, whether she'd still have to go there or whether Elizabeth would be able to sort it out. It all depended on whether or not they believed what she'd told them about Evan. The way her luck was going, it seemed unlikely.

'You broke your wrist once,' Barbara said softly.

'Mum–'

'I don't suppose you remember it. You weren't much older than Samuel. We brought you here, to this very hospital. Such a long time ago now.'

'I didn't know that,' Kate sighed.

'He did it.'

Kate froze. She looked down at Sam. Every detail of him seemed so distinct and clear, and the shape and sound of her breath seemed suddenly loud and uneven. She moved her head slowly, feeling every bone in her neck grind.

'What did you just say?'

Barbara blinked furiously, then met Kate's eyes. She nodded. 'He did it. I can't remember what you were supposed to have done that time, but he was drunk and clumsy and he picked you up and then he dropped you.' She swallowed. 'Ironically, the time he broke your wrist was actually an accident. If you can call it an accident. But that doesn't excuse all the other times. It doesn't excuse how he treated you. Or how often I ignored it.' Her voice cracked at the same moment as her face began to crumple, blurring and melting, tears making tracks down cheeks. 'I denied it, Kate, for all these years. I'm so sorry.'

'Mummy?'

'Hey, sweetheart.' Kate turned to her son and forced herself to smile. Her heart was pounding. 'How are you feeling?'

'Nana crying.'

'I'm fine, Samuel,' Barbara said, wiping her eyes on a handkerchief. 'Just so happy to see you feeling better.'

'Feel funny,' Sam said. He lay back, his bottom lip wobbling. Kate kissed his forehead, then gave him a tumbler of water to sip from.

'The doctor said you might feel a little sicky for a while. We'll wait for him to come and see you again, then you can go home.'

The word hung in the air between them, a hollow sound, full of meaning.

'Why?' she whispered. 'Why did you lie for him? And why are you telling me this here, now?'

Barbara had made an effort to control her tears, but now they started afresh. 'I don't know,' she sobbed. 'Just seeing Sam in pain like that, it brought it all back to me. I remembered you, so helpless, so needy. I let you down, Kate. I wasn't ...' She choked on her words, turning her face away. 'I've been searching my soul to find a way to explain this to you. The truth is, I didn't want it to be true. I thought that if I just ignored it, if I pretended it wasn't happening, then it wouldn't be happening. I wouldn't be that person, married to a man who drank too much and got so angry and did those terrible things to us.' She took a violent, shuddering breath. 'To you.'

'No cry, Nana,' Sam said, reaching out his good arm to pat Barbara's hand. The older woman's skin was mottled and lumpy; Sam's perfect and unblemished. Kate laid her hand on top of Sam's and said nothing. There was a dull throbbing in her head, and her throat was raw, but other than that she felt strangely calm.

'Aren't you going to say anything?' Barbara asked, her eyes pleading. 'I thought you'd be furious with me.'

The throbbing intensified, then died away to a pulse.

'Well, for one thing my son is awake now, so I'm not going to start bawling and arguing with you. We've done enough of that. And for another thing,' Kate paused and thought for a moment, 'I just heard you call him Sam.'

Barbara nodded. 'I found his birth certificate. I've been getting his things ... sorted.'

'Kate?'

Elizabeth's head appeared around the door, her blonde hair falling in curtains on either side of her forthright face. 'I need to talk to you right now. It's important,' she added when Kate demurred.

'What?' Kate said in the corridor, narrowing her eyes. 'What's going on?'

Elizabeth flicked to a page near the back of her notebook. 'The police picked Evan up tonight during a raid in King's Cross.'

'What? I don't understand.'

'I don't have all the details. It was something else, someone they'd been after for a while, but Evan was there and he got caught up in it somehow. Anyway, he was on the system, they knew the police here wanted to question him, so he got taken in.'

'And have they? Have they questioned him?' Kate felt her breath catch in her throat. The social worker nodded. 'And?'

'It was him. The officer said Evan needed to prove his whereabouts that night, he thinks that's the only reason he came clean. But there it is. They're dropping any charges.'

Kate leaned against the wall and looked up at the strip-lit ceiling. 'Could today get any weirder? You won't believe what my mother just said to me.' She waited for Elizabeth to answer, but Elizabeth was still looking at her notebook.

'And the other time?' Kate prompted. 'Back in Manchester? Did Evan confess to that too?'

'That wasn't all he said, Kate,' Elizabeth said with a pained expression. 'He told the officer that leaving the drugs in your bedsit here in Corrin Cove wasn't his idea.'

Kate glanced through the window into Sam's ward. Her mother was talking to him, leaning in, her body language relaxed.

'Who's idea was it?'

Elizabeth followed Kate's gaze. 'He showed them a text.'

Kate nodded. 'Of course he did. He's not stupid. Evan would have kept all her texts. He would never take responsibility for anything if he could help it.'

She watched as her mother turned and smiled wanly through the window. Kate raised her hand and gestured for her to come outside. She steeled herself, allowing all the hope she had felt only moments before to seep out of her body, feeling most of her strength escaping with it. For a second she sank against Elizabeth's arm. The social worker glanced down at her in alarm.

'I'm okay,' Kate said, 'but will you go and sit with Sam for a moment?'

Elizabeth hesitated, but then nodded. 'Go easy,' she

said quietly, passing Barbara in the doorway.

'Are you alright?' Barbara asked. Kate shook her head. When she tried to speak her throat felt raspy, and her voice hardly sounded like her own.

'I didn't get chance to tell you, Mum, but they found drugs in my flat earlier. Just like they did in Manchester.'

'Oh.'

'You don't look well, are you okay?' Kate said through her teeth.

'It's nothing. Carry on.'

'Okay. So, they caught up with Evan tonight. And he told them everything.' Kate leaned closer, close enough to see the thin lines that radiated from her mother's tightly clenched mouth. 'I mean, he told them everything.'

'Kate, I–'

'Don't bother, Mum. There's nothing you could say to make this right.'

'I had nothing to do with what happened in Manchester, you have to believe me.'

'And that makes it okay? You tried to set me up, knowing that after everything that's happened to me, after everything I've been through, there was a good chance I'd get a criminal record for this. Why ...?' Kate stopped, hardly able to speak the words. 'Why do you hate me so much?'

'I don't hate you,' Barbara cried. 'I hate myself. Don't you see? I was a terrible mother, and I was a useless wife. The only thing I've ever been any good at was looking after Samuel. The thought of losing him, it was more than I could bear.'

'So you'd stop at nothing? Nothing. You'd go to any lengths to keep him.'

'Only because I love him so much. Oh, please, Kate. Please don't take him. I know you could, I know you have every reason to hate me, but please don't do it. It's the only home he's ever known. You can visit him every day, you can move in with us if you like. Just don't take my Samuel – my Sam – away from me.'

'Mummy? Nana? What's wrong?'

'Sam, you shouldn't be out of bed.' Kate carefully lifted up her son and cuddled him, throwing Elizabeth an accusing glare over his shoulder. Elizabeth shrugged, unconcerned.

'He's broken his arm, not his legs. And you can discuss all this in court on Friday.'

Kate walked away from her mother's grasping hands and set her son down on the bed. She picked up his teddy and began to play with it, relaxing into Sam's delighted giggles. But when she heard a movement behind her, she spoke again, low and controlled, leaving no room for misunderstanding.

'There will be no histrionics on Friday. I will stand up in court and fight for my son, and I won't need any dirty tricks. No matter what I've done in the past, my love for him will shine through for everyone to see. Now I'd like some time alone with him, before you take him home.'

'Goodbye, Kate,' her mother said. When the door closed softly, Kate didn't turn around.

Chapter 29

Bow Hill looked different in the rain. Glistening and polished, the flat-fronted houses were reflected in puddles, and streetlights sparkled with orange droplets in the night sky. Patrick had to park further down the street than usual, and then he spent a while digging around in the back for an umbrella.

'I know I have one here somewhere,' he said. Kate wasn't bothered about getting wet, but she wasn't in a hurry to get inside either.

'What weather,' Patrick said when he finally gave up and leaned back in his seat with a sigh. 'Every time you and I spend time together it seems to rain.'

'Thanks for the lift home,' Kate said. 'I couldn't face hanging round the hospital, waiting for a cab.'

'It's not a problem.' Patrick held up a supermarket carrier bag. 'You can put this over your head if you like.'

'I'm not so depressed I want to end it all.'

'I didn't mean ... I meant to keep the rain off.'

'I know, I was joking. Sorry. I've never had good timing when it comes to a sense of humour.'

'Me neither. The other day there was this man in the woods, and he said–'

Kate reached up and put her finger to Patrick's lips. The gesture surprised them both, and Kate allowed the feeling of heat that rose inside her core to swell until it spread all through her body. Her fingers tingled with it; her legs felt heavy and far away. 'You've done so much for me,' she told him. 'More than you realise. Just by being there. By being normal.' Her eyes flicked away from his, but not before she had flashed him a look of unmistakable invitation. She got out of the car and crossed the pavement.

This wasn't a night for being alone. This was a night for sinking into the arms of a man who undressed her with such care she might have been the most precious creature in all the world. It was a night for forgetting, but at the same time for remembering – remembering what it was like to come alive inside, to be known by hands that explored and were hungry, and to shout out with joy, knowing only that moment, feeling happy. Feeling wanted.

It was a night to be herself.

***

Early Friday morning, Kate curled up on the floor in her son's room and waited for the sun to rise. In a few hours it would be time to go to court and the waiting would be over.

A knock woke her; she must have fallen asleep. The room was bright now, viciously so, and the shadows thrown from the tree outside made patterns like sharp fingers on the freshly painted walls. Kate stretched out her legs and winced. There was the knock again, and in walked Marie, holding her ubiquitous tray of coffee and biscuits, and getting right down to business.

'Kate, tell me to mind my own beeswax if you want, but I'm here if you need somebody to talk to. Here, drink your coffee. And eat. You need to keep up your strength.'

'I don't feel like eating,' Kate said. But she drank the coffee, feeling it burn her throat the whole way down.

'Don't suppose you do,' Marie agreed amiably. She

was wearing a badly fitting red trouser suit and an orange silk scarf, and her perfume smelt like candyfloss. Kate felt cheered just at the sight of her.

After a few more shots of caffeine, Kate remembered Marie's ordeal at the hands of the police and apologised again.

'It wasn't your fault,' Marie said. 'Besides, my rooms didn't get searched in the end.'

'So you didn't have to show off your artwork?'

Marie gave a rueful grin. 'You can come and have a look sometime if you like. It's quite something.'

'Erm, thanks,' Kate said dubiously. 'So, did Big Tony go for option one or two?'

'Well, it was option one. And the dress was a huge hit, and the restaurant was gorgeous, and he even went down on one knee.'

'You said no, didn't you?'

'My, you do know me well after such a short time. I did, and you know the reason why?'

'Enlighten me.'

'I'm happy as I am. I like having Big Tony around, and he likes dating me. If we got married again, he'd most likely just start playing around again. Leopards never change their spots.'

Kate nodded. She knew Marie was right, but it didn't stop her feeling suddenly choked. It all seemed so hopeless. What was the point in anything if people never changed?

'My mother thinks that about me,' she said. 'I'm a leopard and my spots are drawn on in indelible ink.'

'And maybe you feel that way about her, too?' Marie suggested kindly.

Kate crossed the room and rested her palms on the windowsill. Outside, the October sun cast a brittle light over Bow Hill, and if she leaned forward she could see a sliver of ocean beyond the last of the terrace houses, grey and brown against a pale blue sky.

'She keeps texting me.'

'Your mother?'

'Saying she's sorry. For Sam's accident, for Evan, for everything that happened with my dad.'

'Do you believe her?'

'That she's sorry?' Kate sighed, long and deep. 'I don't know. No, not really. I mean, it's the timing, isn't it? She's saying all this now because she knows she's going to lose Sam.'

'Why now?' Marie asked. 'She's denied it for so long.'

'Sam's accident.' Kate shuddered at the thought of that fractured bone. 'She said it triggered all the memories she's been repressing. All those other "accidents", plus all the times she'd been in hospital herself when I was a kid. She just couldn't deny it any longer.'

'It doesn't bear thinking about, growing up in an environment like that,' Marie said, reaching for another biscuit.

'Not to defend her, but she was terrified of him too. It always started with him getting angry at her about something. His dinner not cooked on time, or her nagging him, or looking at another man, or looking at him the wrong way ...'

'It sure sounds like you're defending her,' Marie pointed out, still eating the biscuit.

'No.' Kate swung away from the window and shook her head. 'I'm not. This isn't about her. And it isn't about me, either. It's not about my dad, or what happened to me as a child. This is about Sam. I shouldn't –'

'What?' Marie stopped chewing. 'Why are you looking like that? What have I said?'

'Nothing.' Kate's face had turned slack; her eyes unfocused. 'I'm just ... I'm just thinking, that's all. I'm just remembering. Something I should have known all along.'

'Now what are you doing?' Marie huffed and followed Kate out of Sam's room, watching with bemused eyes as Kate flung on her navy suit and dragged a brush through her hair. 'We don't need to leave for an hour yet.'

'I've got to do something first,' Kate said distractedly. 'There's stuff I need to ... Oh, where did I put that bag of mine.'

'Kate, take a breath.'

'Marie.' Kate came to rest by the door to her room and laid a hand on her friend's arm. 'Marie, I need to go now. I'll see you later.'

'But where are you going?' Marie cried. 'What are you going to do?'

'Exactly what I should have done all along,' Kate said softly. 'I'm going to put this right.'

Chapter 30

The wind swept across the front of the court building, scattering litter and fallen leaves around Kate's feet. The building's façade was battleship grey, matching both the sky and the wide concrete steps which led up shallowly to the imposing entrance. Kate took the steps two at a time, throwing her bag over her shoulder. She pushed through the doors, ready to be assaulted by noise and bustle, but inside all was quiet.

She looked around for Elizabeth. There was a reception booth on the other side of a vast, echoing space; She jogged over to the desk, calling out Elizabeth's name as soon as she was within earshot.

'If you'll just take a seat, I'll see if she's available.'

Kate sighed in frustration. 'I sent her a message that I needed to see her before the hearing,' she explained to the receptionist, a moustachioed man in his fifties with a nasal voice and the air of someone who has seen it all before. 'I'm sure she's here.'

'Then I'm sure she'll come and find you as soon as she arrives,' he answered, curling up his lip.

Kate gave up and began to prowl the rows of benches lining the public area of the court building. Others were beginning to arrive, little huddles of people, bundled against the cold. She wondered how many of them would be going home today happy, their cases decided in their favour.

'Hey, what's the emergency?'

The social worker emerged from a side door, looking poised and relaxed in a black skirt and white shirt, her long hair tied back smoothly.

'Elizabeth!' Kate fell upon her gladly, a friendly face in a foreign land. 'I need to talk to you. It's important.'

'So I gathered. And this has to happen now? Before the hearing?'

Kate nodded resolutely. 'Yes. It does.'

'I see.' Elizabeth sighed her weary sigh, then gestured for Kate to follow her to a wooden bench that was set against a wall on the far side of the room. She folded her hands in her lap and waited. Kate swallowed, gathering her resolve. This was it. There was no going back now. But it was fine. She knew this was the right thing to do.

If she was honest with herself, she had known it would come to this all along.

Sometimes the truth was just so damned hard to see.

'Do you remember,' she said, 'the day I arrived in Corrin Cove? You said something that day that I should have taken more notice of.'

Elizabeth make a self-deprecating gesture. 'I say a lot of stuff people should take more notice of.'

'I'm sure. But this was to do with Sam. I was complaining about the way Sam's care had been handled – about how he hadn't been brought to see me, and about how I'd been kept in the dark – and you said to me, you said "this isn't about you, Kate, this is about Sam".' Kate sat back and shook her head. 'You shouldn't have had to remind me of that, but you did. And even then it didn't go in. Not fully. All this time I've been telling myself that everything I've done has been in Sam's best interests, but it hasn't been. Not completely. I've been thinking about myself, about what was best for me. Or else I've been thinking about how angry I was with my dad, or my mum, or about how badly I was being treated, how difficult it has been for me.'

'You're being hard on yourself, Kate,' Elizabeth cut in. 'Those things are linked, after all.'

'No, I'm being honest, and it's about time. This was never about Sam, this was about me needing to understand why my father hurt me so badly and never said sorry, and why my mother didn't care enough to ...'

Kate swallowed. She had sworn to herself these past few nights that she wouldn't break down again. She had cried enough already over this. It was over. If there was any kind of line to be drawn here, she had to draw it right now.

She laid her hands on her thighs and smoothed down her skirt. The gesture reminded her of someone. Who was it? Ah, yes. She gave a wry smile and shook her head.

'Elizabeth, I'm going to drop the application to discharge the guardianship order. Instead, I'd like to apply for mediation so that my mother and I can share Sam's care. Maybe he can spend part of the week with her and part of the week with me. I don't know how it will all work out, all I know is he needs stability. He's just lost his granddad, he's just had his mother reappear after a year in a coma, and he needs us all to pull together.'

Kate registered the look on the social worker's face. 'Okay, you can roll your eyes at me, I'll take that. But it's not as if this was being offered from day one and I turned it down. It's not as if my mother has made this easy.'

'Kate,' Elizabeth said, 'believe me, I'm just happy you've come to this decision. I don't care how you got here. The only question now is, are you going to tell your mother, or do you want me to?'

Kate followed Elizabeth's gaze. There, on the other side of the concourse, stood Barbara and Sam.

'She brought him here?' Kate cried. He looked so

small and lost, his hand in his nana's, a woolly hat wedged low on his head.

'She had to,' Elizabeth said quietly.

Kate bit her lip, the full impact of their feud hitting her all over again. Oh, Sam, she thought. Being dragged here to this place so your own family can fight over you as though you were a prize to be won or lost. What have we done to you?

She stood, the sight of her son calling like a beacon.

'Will you tell her?' she said to Elizabeth. 'I need to ... There's a long way to go, for my mother and me. There's still what she did with Evan, and all the rest of the history between us. I just can't talk to her properly, not yet. You understand, don't you?'

'Sure.' Elizabeth stood too, but then she pulled a face and laid her hand on Kate's arm. 'Kate, I'm afraid I haven't been entirely honest with you today.'

'What?' Kate said distractedly. Sam had noticed her now and was waving frantically. She waved back, her face lighting up with the widest grin.

'The thing is, I just wanted to hear what you had to say, and if you hadn't said it – that is, if you hadn't had the chance to say it, I don't think you'd have made the progress you did just now. It was kind of cathartic, don't you think? Coming to that decision?'

'Elizabeth.' Kate turned and regarded her impatiently. 'What are you going on about?'

'The thing is, your mother had already spoken to me before I met with you this morning. She's given up the Special Guardianship Order. Parental responsibility has been restored to you.'

Kate's mouth dropped open. She looked back at Sam, his face picked out so clearly against the backdrop of a milling crowd. He was getting closer now, weaving his way, holding onto his nana's hand, grinning all the way.

And then he was in her arms, her son, her own flesh

and blood, a solid bundle of fierce love, and she held him, pressing her face against his, wiping her tears on his soft, woolly hat.

Chapter 31

November the fifth dawned a clear, crisp day, with just the lightest sprinkling of frost making the beach glint like diamonds in the weak sun. Kate leaned against Patrick and watched three dogs race into the water and out again, their coats slick and glistening. She sighed contentedly, despite the cold. Patrick gripped her more tightly, his body warm at her side. Sometimes he seemed almost able to read her mind. Read this, she thought, imagining his lips on hers, his hands in her hair the way they had been last night, her head tipped back while he kissed her in a frenzy of desire.

'We should be getting back,' he said. 'Sam will be running Marie ragged.'

Kate smiled to herself. Not quite the mind-reader after all.

They trudged back to the promenade, stamping wet sand off their shoes all the way up Bow Hill.

'Are you sure it's going to be safe tonight?' Kate asked for the hundredth time. Patrick rolled his eyes and kissed her lightly on the nose.

'Were you always such a worrywart? It'll be fine. They have this firework display on the beach every year. Sam will love it.'

Kate smiled. She hadn't always been such a worrywart, as he called her, but she was certainly enjoying being one now.

Back at the house, Marie and Sam were playing in the

tiny back garden. The arrival of Sam had prompted the removal of all of Big Tony's 'artwork'; now Kate, Sam and Patrick were regular visitors to Marie's ground floor rooms, and this was where Sam often played, watched over by a doting Marie while Kate worked at her sewing machine upstairs, altering clothes and making curtains, her fledgling business already thriving. Kate had moved her chair right next to the window so she could enjoy the sight as well as the sound of Sam, who loved to be outside in all weathers. No matter how tired she became, no matter how hard she had to work to keep the money flowing in, the presence of Sam was a balm to her soul.

'Kate,' Marie called, waving from the garden. Sam was playing in the sandpit, building castles and then knocking them down with squeals of delight. 'Come and taste my new coffee mocha recipe. I'm trying it out for tonight.'

'See you later,' Patrick whispered.

'Later,' Kate said, turning to watch him go.

***

The coffee mocha was a great success, as was Marie's hot chocolate with marshmallows, which they carted down to the beach in great insulated tubs, ready to share with the hordes of friends Marie and Patrick had arranged to meet for the Corrin Cove fireworks extravaganza. Kate and Marie sipped their drinks and watched Sam play with a group of boys from the neighbourhood, the older children holding sparklers aloft in the night air.

'He seems to be settling into his new routine fine,' Marie remarked.

'He's adapted well,' Kate agreed, wrapping her gloved hands around her mug. 'The first few weeks were tricky, but we've worked through it.'

'And you'll keep going like this? Half the week at Bow Hill, the other half at your mum's?'

'I don't know what the future holds, Marie,' Kate said honestly. 'I'm just taking it one day at a time.'

'Are things any better? With you and your mum, I mean?'

Kate shook her head. One of Marie's friends appeared, gushing approval for the hot chocolate, and Kate smiled automatically, then turned away, glad of the distraction. She wondered what her father would have made of the way things had turned out. She held her cup to her face and let the steam warm her cheeks, feeling the sudden tears dry on her skin as quickly as they'd appeared.

'Not so close to the bonfire, Sam,' she called, but it was only to reassure herself. He was surrounded by other children, and the bonfire was only a spluttering campfire at least twenty metres along the beach.

'Hi there, worrywart.' His breath was soft against her hair and she could hear the smile in his voice.

She rested her head against Patrick's shoulder and allowed the feeling of contentment to flow through her body. How long had it been since she'd felt like this, free from guilt and pain and regret? Too long, she decided. There was no point hoping for any more miracles. Getting Sam back had been enough of a miracle. That things might improve with her mother, that they might even reconcile one day, would certainly be a miracle too far.

'You look chilly,' Patrick said. 'I'll get you another hot chocolate.'

'It was coffee,' Kate called after him, but he was already striding away up the beach. She pulled a face, and turned back towards the sea, tugging her coat more tightly around her. There, standing close enough to touch, was her mother.

'Mum!' Kate was so surprised she couldn't speak for what felt like a full minute. Her mother didn't seem to know what to say either. She shifted from foot to foot and folded her arms across her body, then dropped them to her side.

'Kate.'

Barbara took a deep breath, and Kate noticed that her hands were trembling. 'I've come to …' She halted, took another steadying breath, then finally seemed to pull herself together. 'Kate, I'm here so that I can …' Her mouth clamped shut again and she looked away, but not before Kate had noticed the tears swelling in her eyes.

'It's okay, Mum,' said Kate wearily. 'I understand. You want to see Sam enjoying the fireworks. We don't have to stick to our days so rigidly. And you can talk to me when I come to pick him up, you know. You don't have to be so formal about it.'

'No, it's not that.' Barbara reached inside her handbag and pulled out a stick. It was gnarled with flaking bark, the kind Kate might have picked off the ground in Patrick's wood. 'Of course I'd love to see Samuel,' she said, 'but what I really came for was to give you this.'

Kate stared at the twig, puzzled. 'You came here to give me that?'

Barbara nodded, her face twisted in embarrassment. 'It seemed a good idea at the time.' She tried to laugh, but her laughter faded into nothing. 'It was supposed to be an olive branch.'

'An olive branch?' Kate looked again at the stick her mother clutched in her pale fingers. And then she understood. 'So what is it, really?'

Her mother pulled a wry face. 'It's actually a piece of your father's hedge.'

At the mention of her father Kate stiffened. But her mother only smiled sadly and held out her hand. 'Will you take it?' she said in a small voice. 'I've been so stupid, Kate. I'm a stupid old lady, and I was proud and stubborn and afraid. I thought I would be lonely without Samuel.' She corrected herself, keeping her watery eyes trained on Kate's face. 'I mean without Sam. And that was true. But the person I was missing all along was my own daughter, the daughter I'd let down so badly. And I'm so sorry. So very, very sorry.'

But Kate couldn't let her say any more. She pulled her mother close, noticing how frail and brittle she felt, how small she seemed in her arms. Barbara stepped out of Kate's embrace and held her daughter with both hands. 'You did nothing wrong, Kate,' she said, stepping back so Kate could see her face clearly. 'Your father and I, we didn't give you the best start in life. All that happened to you, it was not your fault.' She smiled then, the smile turning her into the woman whose love Kate had craved for so long.

'Nana!'

Sam bowled into them, one chubby fist clutching a half-eaten hot dog, his face smeared with tomato ketchup.

'Oh, my goodness,' Kate exclaimed.

'Someone's having a good time,' Barbara laughed.

'There's sparklers, Nana, come see. Come see!'

'Do you mind?'

Kate smiled and shook her head. 'Have fun,' she told them. 'Sam, take care of your nana. Make sure she doesn't get lost.'

She turned around to find Patrick eyes upon her.

'I got your coffee,' he said softly.

'Did you know she was coming tonight?' Kate asked, still watching her son and her mother as they weaved their way down to the shore.

Patrick didn't answer her at once. He moved to her side and pulled her against him. It was, she decided, one of her favourite places to be.

'It's like foresting,' he said. 'Sometimes, it's a good idea to let nature take its course. But sometimes, you need to step in and lend a helping hand.'

Kate narrowed her eyes. 'Are you always this wise?'

'Oh, yes. And later, I'll be expecting you to show me just how grateful you are.'

'I might just do that,' she said, waving at Sam, who was tipping wet sand all over her mother's shoes. 'But first we've got a fireworks display to watch.'

'Oh, fireworks,' Patrick said blithely. 'Well, if it's fireworks you're after, you've certainly come to the right place.'

THE END

Acknowledgements

There are so many people who helped with the development and writing of this book, it's hard to know where to start. First of all my thanks go, as always, to my husband, who is endlessly supportive and positive, even when writing takes me away from the family and makes me grouchy. To my beta readers, Pauline, Emma D, Emma H, Mandy, Poppy, and Rachel, thank you so much for your feedback and comments. A special thank you to the RNA reader who gave such a thorough and bracing edit - this book wouldn't be what it is without your input! My thanks go to Kristy for her expert advice, and to the wonderful Internet for such a wealth of research resources. Information about the court system was correct at the time of writing and any errors are mine alone. Thanks as well to Jude White for her most excellent proofreading services, and Chris Howard for the paperback cover. And finally, thank you to my readers for inspiring me to keep going and keep on writing!

To find out more about my books, visit me at www.joannephillips.co.uk where you can sign up for my newsletter and hear about new releases, giveaways and special promotions.